WITCH HILL

Marcus Sedgwick works in children's publishing, and before that was a bookseller. He is also a stone carver and wood engraver. His first novel, *Floodland*, came out last year and was hailed as 'a dazzling debut from a new writer of exceptional talent' in *Publishing News*. He lives in Sussex.

WITCH HILL

Marcus Sedgwick

Illustrations by the author

Dolphin Paperbacks

By the same author

Floodland

First published in Great Britain in 2001
as a Dolphin Paperback
by Orion Children's Books
a division of the Orion Publishing Group
Orion House
5 Upper St Martin's Lane
London WC2H 9EA

Reprinted 2001, 2002

A catalogue record for this book is available
from the British Library.

ISBN 1 85881 883 4

Typeset at The Spartan Press Ltd,
Lymington, Hants
Printed in Great Britain by
The Guernsey Press Co. Ltd, Guernsey, C.I.

Darling Alice
I love you
Daddy

Contents

1

By the Pricking of my Thumbs

Fear gripped my guts like tangled twine. I woke, eyes searching at the darkened window, ears straining for the sound of footsteps outside. But all I could hear was my pounding heart, and I shrank back into bed, still afraid. Still terrified.

I'd never had a nightmare like this before. Not really, not even after the fire. I'd had bad dreams, who doesn't? But you wake up and it's all okay. Now I knew what it was to wake from a deep sleep and still be afraid long after the nightmare is over. I stared into the darkness, not daring to move. It felt as though there wasn't enough air in the room. I struggled, gasping for breath. I just could *not* breathe. It was as if there was something else in the room, using up *my* air.

I wanted someone to tell me it was all right, but I was still too scared to get out of bed. Besides, I didn't fancy waking my aunt in the middle of the night. I'd only been at her house a couple of days – I didn't want to start freaking her out on top of everything else.

I cowered under the bedcovers, trying to stop panicking. I forced myself to move my arm far enough to put the bedside light on. That helped. With the darkness gone I seemed to be able to breathe a little easier.

Then there was a knock at the door. I must have yelped because a voice said something.

"Are you all right?"

I calmed down a bit. I realised that monsters probably don't knock before they eat you, and anyway I recognised the voice. It was Alison, my cousin.

"Come in," I said. I was pleased I hadn't woken my aunt, but Alison was, like her, sort of weird. It wasn't the way she looked . . . I can't really explain – she's older than me; I barely know her. At least, I didn't know her then.

"Are you all right?" she said again. "Jamie?"

"There was . . . I had a bad dream. That's all."

"Sounded quite bad, you were yelling."

Then my aunt stuck her head round the door. I *had* woken her, after all.

"What's going on?"

"It's all right," said Alison. I was grateful to her for taking over.

"I thought someone was being murdered . . . are you mucking about?"

"Mum! He had a nightmare. Go back to bed. I'll see he's okay."

Alison turned back to me. She and my aunt Jane seemed more like sisters to each other, not mother and daughter. Jane sniffed and went back to bed. She was always tired. She had been up late, working in the pub in the village.

2

"Shall I put the big light on?" Alison asked.

I nodded.

"Want to tell me about it?"

Yes, I thought, I do. Even though, as I said, Alison was a little strange, I wanted to talk to someone about the dream. I didn't want to go back to sleep for a while at least. I didn't even stop to think how odd it was that she was taking any interest in me – in the few days I'd been at the house she'd barely spoken to me. She was always on the phone to her friends, working out how they were going to spend the Easter holidays. I'd guessed there was some boy she was interested in too, and she was trying to get her friends to ask him out for her. It seemed to take up most of her time.

"Go on then," she said.

I didn't think I'd said anything, but she seemed to know I was going to tell her anyway.

"It was awful. I was in bed, just like I . . . am now. I can't explain really, because I was in bed here, but I was outside too."

I looked at Alison, but her face showed nothing. I looked at the bedcovers and went on. I couldn't think how to explain it, but then something became a bit clearer.

"I think . . . I was in bed, but my mind was outside, sort of *exploring*. My body was still here, but my mind was down in the valley somewhere. Then I came up through the village and the wood and onto the hill. The hill above the village. And then . . ."

"Then?"

"It's scary. Sorry."

Alison looked concerned. Genuinely concerned.

3

"It might help."

"I was up on the hill for a while. I think I was looking for something and then . . . there was a woman. A horrible, scary old woman."

I saw a flicker in Alison's eyes.

"Go on."

"She was really, really old, and all sort of shrivelled up, and . . . she was on the hill somewhere, I think. Somewhere dark . . . I found her. She found me. I don't know, but we . . . *touched*. Once she knew I was there, that was it. Once she knew I existed, there was no way of undoing it. She came for me, here, in my bed. My mind was back here straight away, but it was too late. She knew I was here and she was unstoppable. I could see her through the window; a black thing on the hillside, coming for me. The way she moved was horrible. She was hobbling, but sort of running too. Shambling. And she moved so fast. She was coming over the hill, and I knew she was coming right for me. Nothing would stop her."

I hesitated. I knew I'd been gabbling, and Alison was wrong; talking about it wasn't helping me at all. It was making me scared again.

"Go on," said Alison.

"That's it really."

"But what happened? Did she . . . ?"

"No!" I yelled. I tried to calm down. "I woke up. When I saw her moving like that, coming for me, I tried to get up, but I couldn't. I couldn't move a muscle. It was as though I was paralysed, or something. That's when I lost it and started screaming."

4

"I heard."

"I'm sorry."

"No, that's all right. Not your fault, is it? Anyway, you feel better now, don't you? Helps to talk about these things."

I nodded, but I didn't feel that much better. I just felt stupid, and though I was still scared, I suddenly wanted her to go.

"Want a drink or anything?"

"Yes," I said, "but I can get it."

"Sure?"

"Yes," I said. "I'm only going downstairs."

I got out of bed to prove it. She seemed to be convinced.

"Well, sleep well. No more dreams. See you." She headed for her room.

"See you in the morning," I said, and started to go down the hall.

As soon as I heard her door close, I turned round and went straight back to bed. I was just about to climb in when I noticed something. The bedroom carpet. There were very faint white footprints on the floor. Wondering who had made them, I knelt down for a closer look. As I did so a disturbing thought began to creep up my neck and into the back of my brain. I knew whose footprints they were. I sat on the bed and pulled my foot right up under the bedside light. I was right. The soles of my feet were covered with white stuff. I felt it with my fingertips.

It was chalk.

First, it is said that she learned this detestable art of witchcraft at the age of twelve, and that she at that time did renounce God and gave of her blood to Sathan.

Then, that she did from this time employ the said detestable art for the conjuration and invocation of evil and wicked spirits for sorcerous purposes for a period of not less than five years.

And, that she did that March exercise her enchantments upon Richard Sedley, of Frog End, Ashbury as revenge for the quarrel between them, and that the said Richard Sedley began to pine and waste and thus he was consumed until his death April second, the year of Our Lord, 1658.

2

The Thing on the Hill

I got back to sleep in the end, but only when day had started to come. The daylight seemed to take the edge off my fear, and then exhaustion took over.

I don't know why, but darkness is frightening. Or at least, it can be. When I finally did wake up, it was odd. I must have been really out of it. Sometimes when you wake up, you can't remember where you are. Once or twice, I've woken up and for a second or two couldn't remember *who* I was.

This time it was worse. I couldn't remember *what* I was. If that sounds stupid . . . all I know is that I lay in bed, with my eyes open, but saw nothing. Time passed. I know that. I knew too that I was a living thing, but that was about it. My brain was running, but with no thoughts. I felt as though I was an animal. A dog, no, not a dog. Something more primitive, something barely conscious. Something that thought simple, basic thoughts. Evil thoughts.

It felt as if something had been inside my brain for a bit;

using it, wanting it and living inside it. And I had woken up while it was still there and caught it.

Then it started to pass. I remembered I was human. Then I remembered I was a human called James Fraser. Then I remembered I was a human called James Fraser who was spending the Easter holidays with his aunt, because his own house had burnt down. I remembered being sent down to my Aunt Jane's house in the West Country even before school had finished. My friends had been jealous and had given me stick about it, but they hadn't been through what I'd been through. The fire. They had *no* idea.

I got up, something bothering me all the time.

I dressed slowly, ducking under the low part of the sloping ceiling to find a pair of socks I had thrown there, gazing out of the window. Aunt Jane's house is old. The sort of old house where you nearly hit your head all the time and you have to crouch down to see out of the upstairs windows. Right then I didn't bother, but just stared down through the window, so that all I could see was a bit of the back garden behind the house. I knew if I bent down I would have a view of all of the back garden, and then the fields, which run right up to the hill above the village of Crownhill. But I didn't.

All the time there was something scratching at the back of my mind. Halfway down the stairs to the kitchen I remembered what it was – the nightmare. It hit me fast and hard. I suddenly felt I couldn't breathe again. I sat on the stairs, trying to calm down, waiting for my breath to come back, and that's how I overheard Alison talking to Aunt Jane. They didn't know I was there.

It sounded as if they were having an argument. I wasn't really concentrating. I was trying to get the picture of my nightmare out of my head, but it was like an itch that you can't stop scratching. My brain kept showing me that old woman coming for me across the hillside.

"Well, you explain it then," said Alison. She was coming through the back door into the kitchen.

"Alison, don't start," said my aunt. She sounded cross.

"It can't be a coincidence," Alison said, ignoring her.

"He's just a boy, and it was just a dream."

And that's when I started listening. I mean really listening. They were talking about me. There was something in the way Aunt Jane said 'just a boy' I didn't like. But it made me want to hear more.

"Exactly!" said Alison.

"No, Alison, not 'exactly'. It doesn't mean anything. It . . . he had a dream."

"He had *the* dream."

"He had a bad dream, and that's all. Now I've got too much organising to do for Sunday, and I want everything to go smoothly. As smoothly as possible. It's too important. It's been hard enough to get the permission and get people behind it. The last thing I want is to run out of sandwiches. So just drop it."

"But Mum, this could be important, too."

"Now!" hissed Jane. She meant it.

There was silence. I was sure Alison was trying to decide whether or not to say something. I could feel my heart beating. I shifted my weight on the stairs and they creaked under me. It's an old house, old stairs do that. I was sure they'd heard me, but I got away with it.

"Okay, Mum," said Alison.

"That's a good girl," said Jane.

"Mum, I'm sixteen!"

"Okay, sorry. Now are you going to help me get ready?"

I crept back upstairs as quietly as possible and only set off a couple of floorboards. Then I came back down noisily, pretending nothing had happened. I knew something had.

I could probably have said, casually, "was that me you were talking about?" But I didn't. I had heard the tension in Jane's voice. The anger. But that was only a part of it. The rest of it . . . I'm not sure.

What stuck in my mind more was that Alison had interrupted her mother. "Just a dream," Jane had said, and Alison had corrected her. "*The* dream," she said.

The dream.

"James!" said Jane, seeing me come into the kitchen. "Good morning."

I expected Alison to follow this up with some crass remark about it only just being morning, but she didn't. She hovered in the doorway for a moment, staring at me. She had a strange expression on her already strange face. It was a mixture of concern and . . . was it envy?

She slipped out of the door.

"Don't worry about her," Jane said, seeing the look on my face. "It's only natural you'll need a bit more sleep, after the trouble you've had."

I didn't need her to talk about "the trouble I'd had", but

she went on to other things and I was glad. Just a minute before, the tone of her voice had been quite different. Now it was so sweet; I couldn't believe the sudden change. It didn't seem right, somehow.

"Oh, but what would you like for breakfast?" she went on, "Dear me! What would Sarah say?"

Sarah's my mum. I thought that Mum probably had other things to worry about. Like sorting everything out after the fire, for starters. She wouldn't be bothering about whether my breakfast was on time.

"Have a seat there, by the range."

Jane pointed to a chair by the huge, old stove. Even though it was April, there was a fire in. I looked at it, and chose a seat at the table instead.

"Eggs?" she asked.

"Fine," I said, but what I was thinking was, "*the* dream", "*the* dream".

While I ate my breakfast, Alison and Jane came and went in the kitchen. It was an old cottage, probably several hundred years old. The kitchen was one of those amazing country kitchens – not very big, but all beams and pots and pans hanging on them. A high shelf ran around near the top of the wall, and it was loaded with all sorts of bits and pieces. Little wooden carvings, some of which were quite odd, and strange woven basket things, called corn dollies, I think. There was even a stuffed bird. A wren, maybe, because it was so tiny. There were small stones; smooth pebbles with holes right through them. And there were other things too, I had no idea what some of them were.

Alison and Jane were preparing lots of food. I knew Jane had been planning some event. I knew it was taking place on Sunday, but I hadn't really taken much notice. Both of them were making a big show of getting all the food ready for whatever it was that was happening. I wished I'd listened, because now I didn't know and I knew they knew I didn't know. Which made it even more irritating.

In the end I had to ask.

"What's going on? I didn't quite catch it, before."

"What? Oh this."

I could tell Alison was pleased I'd asked.

"It's for the Scouring, isn't it. I thought Mum told you all about it when you got here."

She had. But I'd only just got off the eight-hour coach journey from home when she told me. I wasn't really listening. There were other things on my mind. Other things *in* my mind, like burnt houses and waving goodbye to my family.

I could have stayed. I could have helped, but Mum wouldn't let me. Said I needed a break from it all. Considering what had happened. The fire, and with Kizzie, and everything.

"Oh," I said.

Alison went on pootling about.

I waited for a proper explanation, but she didn't say anything, so I had to ask again.

"Tell me again, the Scouring is . . . ?"

"The Scouring of the crown."

"Ah," I said.

14

"Yes. It's been a while, you see."

"Oh."

I knew what the crown was at least. It was what gave the village its name – Crownhill. But it was only then that I made any connection with . . . that I made any connection.

The crown was a large drawing on the hill above the village, made by cutting the turf away to reveal the white of the chalk underneath.

Chalk.

Mum had told me about the crown before I came down on the coach.

Apparently, I had seen it once before, when I was two. I can't remember anything about that visit. The only other time I'd been down here. The family isn't that close. In both senses of the word. Strange, though, that my mum and Aunt Jane look very alike.

I'd had a shock when Jane picked me up from the coach station. For a second I thought Mum had beaten me down here somehow and was waiting for me. Then I realised it was my aunt. It took while to shake the feeling. They share the same messy blonde hair.

My mum and Jane get on okay, sort of, but it's a long way from the West Country to Lancashire, where I live. Where I used to live until my house burnt down.

If I had known then, when I was two, that I wouldn't come back to Crownhill for about a decade, then I suppose I might have paid more attention.

In those ten years, Jane and Alison had moved away

15

from Crownhill. Alison's father had got a job abroad. Germany, I think, and they'd gone too. About three years ago Alison and her mum moved back, but even then Jane and *my* mum had remained distant.

"It's supposed to look like a crown, see?" my mum said. "But you'd have a job knowing if you weren't told. It's just a blob really. Not like the other hill-carvings around there. There's a lovely horse near Swindon, and then there's that naughty giant."

That was all she'd said. I'd seen a photo of the "naughty giant" at school, so I knew why she didn't tell me any more about it.

But the crown of Crownhill was just a bit of a mess that was supposed to look like a crown, and which was made of chalk. Chalk.

When Jane's back was turned, I glanced under the table, trying to look at the soles of my feet.

"What are you doing, Jamie?" said Alison from the door, an empty box in her hands. I shrugged. I couldn't see anything now, but there had definitely been chalk on my feet the night before. I was sure of it. Well, I think I was sure. Sometimes it's hard to remember what's a dream and what's real. Later on, I mean. Usually a few years have to go by for you to get things like that muddled up. This time it seemed to have happened overnight.

"So what are you doing to the crown, then?" I asked.

"*Scouring* it," said Alison.

"Well, yes, but apart from that?"

Alison smiled.

"It just means we're going to clean it up a bit, that's all. It used to be done every seven years, but it hasn't been done for years. Decades. We're going to give it the best clean it's had in a century! Mum's got the whole village going now. Well, maybe half of it, anyway."

A funny look crossed her face, but Jane didn't notice. She was obviously enjoying this praise from her daughter. I could tell that, even though she had her back to me at the sink, where she was doing some washing up.

"She's persuaded the parish council and Historic England and got a committee together, too. There's only really a few of the villagers who don't . . ." she stopped. Then, "You *are* going to help, too, aren't you Jamie?"

"Oh, yes," I said automatically. I hadn't really thought about it. I'd no idea what it was all about, but it would be something to do, at least.

They went on with their preparations. They seemed to be making about a million sandwiches. I thought it might actually be fun to help with the Scouring; it had been pretty boring so far. Until the dream, that is.

Anyway, I wanted a closer look at the chalk carving. I suppose it was possible I'd been sleepwalking. Anything's possible. Isn't it?

Something occurred to me.

"So who made it in the first place?"

"What, James?"

"The crown," I said. "Who made it in the first place?"

I thought it was a simple question, but the look that passed between Jane and Alison was weird.

After a while, in which each of them seemed to be waiting for the other to tell me, Alison answered.

"Well, it's the name of the village, you see? The village is named after the crown."

That wasn't what I'd asked. I tried again.

"But who actually made it?"

Again, there was the same reaction. I suddenly regretted asking the question.

"Well," said Alison, "they say it was carved on the hill after the Civil War. The villagers were Royalists mostly. At least, they were after Charles II was restored to the throne, I suppose. And so they carved a huge crown on the hillside to show their loyalty to the king."

It took me a moment to work out what was wrong with what she'd said.

"So the village was built after the crown was, then?"

Silence, again.

"Otherwise, the village couldn't have been named after the crown, could it?"

"That's true," said Alison, quietly.

"But then who were the villagers if the village didn't exist yet?"

My cousin looked at my aunt, but Jane still had her back to us, washing a bowl. I was sure I'd seen her wash it once already.

"Unless," said Alison suddenly, "the village was always called Crownhill, and they just thought it would be a good idea to make the carving to show it off. That seems more likely, doesn't it? Mum?"

Jane nodded.

"Yes," she said. It could do. Whatever."

I finished my breakfast quietly, wondering what on earth I'd asked.

That the girl did, in a further pact with Sathan, take on the possession of a familiar — a devil in animal form.

This familiar was in the shape of a cat, named Chub, and she did use this cat for her evil purposes.

This cat, Chub, did, on her instruction, undertake to kill the pigs of Elizabeth Stoke, for revenge of her calling the girl a witch.

This devil in the shape of a cat did also kill the horse of Robert Black, and turn the milk of his cows sour, for revenge of him calling the girl a wanton.

And thus it was this Chub which was vital to the girl for her killing of Richard Sedley. These are the ways of the familiar.

3

Dead Kings

It was over twenty-four hours since I'd had my nightmare. I'd had a totally normal night's sleep on Saturday night. I was walking through the village on a lovely sunny Sunday morning. So why, at the back of my mind, was something eating away at me?

I walked slowly, still limping a little on my bad leg. I'd hurt it when I'd jumped from the window.

I walked past an old stone building called The Red Barn and a tree stump on the green with knots like an old face. I sensed things all around me. I heard the patter of the water running under the bridge on the way into the village. I saw dark shadows in the woods, and I felt something stirring, deep underground, but not far away. I walked on, and saw the pub come into view across the green.

That's where I was going. The pub. Jane had asked me to take a message to Robin Hunt, the landlord of the King's Head.

Yes, I thought, it would have to be a King's Head. It must have been named after Charles II was put on the throne. I tried to remember when the Civil War ended, and how long Oliver Cromwell ruled for. We'd been doing it in history that term, but I couldn't remember.

Since the fire, I hadn't learnt anything. That was why they told me to take the rest of the term off. So I'd spent a couple of weeks knocking around doing nothing, until Mum and Dad decided it would be better if I came down to stay with Jane and Alison for a while. Why I couldn't have gone to stay with one of my mates from school, I don't know. They, Mum and Dad that is, wanted me to get right away from everything. Well, you can run away, but your mind comes with you, doesn't it? And all the memories in it come too.

Make a fresh start in the summer, they said at school. What did they know? It's not that easy; I knew it wasn't going to be, why didn't they? You don't wake up in your bed with your house on fire and forget it in a week or two. You at one end of the hall and your mum and dad's bedroom at the other, and flames roaring up the stairway between you.

And little Kiz . . .

It's not that easy to forget something like that.

But the nightmare had scared me almost more than the fire. Two days later, and I was still scared, when I thought of that old woman hobbling over the hill towards me, at an unnerving speed.

I stopped outside the King's Head. Aunt Jane worked part-time in the pub, it was the only money she and Alison had coming in. Alison's granddad, who lived a couple of doors away, was retired and didn't seem to do anything much. He spent most evenings in the King's Head making his pint last all night. Alison was full of talk of finding a well-paid job as soon as she left school, but I couldn't see where. There was nothing much around.

I looked at the sign for the pub. It was the same thing you get for a King's Head everywhere. I'd seen it before. Not this one, but a dozen like it. An oak tree with the head and shoulders of King Charles looming out of the middle. And of course, that meant that he would have hidden in that very oak tree down on the village green, along with all the other oak trees on all the other village greens he's supposed to have hidden in.

People are so stupid, I thought. I had another try at remembering when the Civil War ended. All I could remember was that it was sixteen-something or other. The middle of the seventeenth century anyhow. Well, there was no way that oak tree was that old. It was at least a hundred years old, maybe a bit more than that, but not three hundred years old. But I bet that didn't stop people in the pub believing the story when they'd had a drink or two.

Come to think of it, I couldn't even remember which Charles was supposed to have hidden in the tree, Number One or Number two. I decided it didn't make any difference.

Well, not after all this time anyway.

The pub was shut. Of course it would be shut; it was Sunday morning. There wasn't the slightest sign of anyone around.

"Just bang on the door," Aunt Jane had told me.

So I did.

Nothing happened. I peered through a small dark window at the front. It looked as if it hadn't opened in years, and I couldn't see anything through it either. I had the vague sense of things moving in the reflections on the glass, but when I turned around, there was no one behind me. Just the trees swaying on the green. I decided to knock again, but before I could a window slid open above my head.

"What do you want?"

I knew straight away that it was Robin. He was quite old – I hadn't a clue exactly how old, just old. And he was large. His head and shoulders filled the window.

"Well, what do you want?"

And he was grumpy – that much Jane had told me.

"I've got a message for you."

I waited for him to say something, but he only scowled.

"From Jane, I'm her nephew and . . ."

"Just the message," he barked.

"Oh yes. She said to say that she won't be able to work this evening after all. She says she'll be too busy after the Scouring to get here on time."

"I knew it," Robin said. He was close to falling out of the window at this point. I was glad he was upstairs and not on the pavement with me.

"She said to say . . ."

"She's very sorry, yes, I know, I've heard it before. Why I go on putting up with her I don't know. Her father spends more time in this pub than she does. Might as well stick him behind the bar."

26

He went on like this for a while, ignoring me, glowering at the village green and getting more and more worked up. He was practically shouting too. I hoped no one was watching – it was all quite embarrassing.

"And where am I supposed to find someone now?"

He didn't show any sign of stopping, and still seemed to have forgotten that I was there. I started to drift away, but then he directed his attention at me again.

"Couldn't have told me this before now, I suppose? Hmm? Not what you'd call convenient, is it? Ever since she got this idea about scouring the old woman into her head she's thought about nothing else."

I couldn't fail to notice that.

Even though I had barely been listening, and he was talking on fast forward, those three words stuck out as if they were underlined in red pen.

"Excuse me," I said, my voice wavering. And it wasn't him I was scared of either.

He stopped.

"What?"

"What did you say?"

"What?"

"You said, scouring 'the old woman'."

"So?"

"Well, I thought it was a crown."

He hesitated.

"That's what I said," he said.

The boldness of this obvious lie took a moment to sink in.

"You said . . ." I began.

"Don't you contradict me."

"But . . ."

"Now clear off, and tell your aunt I've had it with her!"

I didn't care if he yelled at me now.

"Tell her yourself."

"And just when am I going to get the pleasure of seeing her?"

"Well, you'll be at the Scouring like everyone else, won't you?"

"No, I won't be, so push off."

The window slammed down.

"Everything okay with Robin?" Jane asked when I got back to the cottage.

"Oh, fine," I said. She didn't notice the sarcasm in my voice, and I thought she wouldn't care anyway, so I dropped it.

"Good," she said.

I had to admit that Robin was right. Jane was so wrapped up with getting everything ready for the Scouring that she was taking no notice of anything else. Not for the first time I wondered what was so important about it. It just seemed like a nice day out. A picnic on the hill, with a bit of gardening thrown in. Most of the village was going to be there. Maybe all of it. Well, all except Robin.

He had every right to be annoyed with Jane letting him down at such short notice too, which only made it more irritating that he was so nasty. The way that he had lied to me, when it was clear to both of us that he was, had upset me too. He had treated me as though he was talking to an idiot. I thought about asking Jane why he'd called 'it' 'the old woman', but now was not the time. She was whizzing around the kitchen in a flurry of last-minute panic. Then she stopped.

"Well, come on James, are you ready? It's time we were on the hill."

It was nearly half-past nine.

Alison had left already – things weren't supposed to start properly until ten, but she'd left just after eight, even though it only took five minutes to get onto the hill, and another ten to get to the crown.

From the back of the house you couldn't really see anything of the crown at all. Jane had said she was sure it would look better when we cleaned it up. No, as I think about it, what she actually said was "different".

I still don't know if she really knew what was going to happen.

The best view of the carving was from the far side of the village green, at the other end from the King's Head. But even from there, it still only looked like a random mess of lines and curves. And they weren't chalk-white lines either. The chalk had gone a dirty green colour from being left so long exposed to the air, and the whole thing was overgrown with brambles and nettles. It had been years since anyone had done what we were about to do.

Jane and I pushed through the old rotting gate at the bottom of her garden. It was really the top, because the garden sloped up away from the house. Her garden was the beginning of the hill itself. Jane liked that.

29

"There's nature right on your doorstep," she said, a little bit too often.

The hill stretched out before us, with all its dark secrets hidden underground.

There were other people joining us now. Jane waved to them, smiling, calling "Good morning". She was enjoying it again. She loved the fact that all this was her doing. She seemed unbelievably annoying to me, but everyone waved back and said what luck it was that there was going to be good weather.

"Not luck," Jane mumbled to me as we trudged up the hill.

"What?" I said.

"Not luck. About the weather. It can't rain today, you see? It's too important. No such thing as luck, anyway."

"Right," I said, and pretended to be out of breath.

Though Jane was revelling in all the fuss, I couldn't help wonder what would happen when she next went to work at the King's Head. *If* she still had a job by then. I imagined Robin would bring her down to earth, fast. I wondered why he hadn't fired Jane already. I couldn't imagine her as a barmaid.

And then we were on the hill.

The hill, where, in my dream two nights before, I had seen the . . . witch.

For the first time, *the word* entered my head.

It seems obvious now, but until that point I swear I hadn't even thought it.

Witch.

That was what I had found, in my mind, up on the dark, lonely hill. I had roamed around, rummaging across the hillside, and I had peered into places I shouldn't have. I had disturbed an old woman, an old woman who was an ancient, foul, evil witch. She chased me, she nearly got me.

But only in my dreams.

Dreams.

I shuddered, despite the warmth of the sunny morning.

"All right, Jamie?"

Aunt Jane looked at me, and I realised I was standing motionless on the hill. I was being silly, I decided. It was a beautiful sunny morning. Late April, with flowers bursting open everywhere. It was stupid to be scared of it all. In the daytime, things that happen at night just don't seem real. Like your house burning. That was something else that didn't seem real any more. The smoke, the flames, the shouting; it all seemed like something I'd watched on TV. I knew it wasn't though, or I wouldn't be here.

"Just my leg," I said, and walked on. Jane knew that I'd hurt it when I jumped from the window, and it was a useful excuse.

"We'll go more slowly. Sorry."

It wasn't far to the crown; about ten minutes slow walk up one of the many sheep tracks that wound around the hill.

31

To the side of us was Crown Wood, which covered the shoulders of the hill like a dark green cape, leaving only the head exposed.

The face that looked down onto the village was mostly bare, apart from grass and scrub, and a few brambles, which suddenly thickened as we turned from the sheep track sideways along the hill.

"Here we are," Jane said.

"Where?" I asked.

"Look, there's Alison!"

Alison sprang up from behind a particularly big patch of nettles and weeds.

I realised that we were standing on the crown.

At my feet, what I had thought was a dirty old sheep track now turned out to be part of the chalk lines.

"Don't stand on the carving, will you?" said Alison, as she came over.

I was about to ask why not. Then she smiled.

"Sorry. Look, let's start. I've brought some tough gloves for you. There's nettles and brambles everywhere."

"They seem worst just where the carving is, don't they?" I said.

"Typical!" said Jane cheerily, and slapped me on the back. "Anyway, we can't start yet. We've got to wait for the woman from Historic England."

"Do we have to?" said Alison. She looked a little awkward – I guessed she might have been at it already.

Jane paused.

"For the hundredth time, yes," she said, sternly. "Anyway, there aren't enough people here yet. I'll only have to keep explaining things over and over again. We said ten, so we'd better wait until then at least."

"And then we'll start whether that woman comes or not?"

"Possibly."

There were quite a few people gathering, and suddenly, just before ten o'clock, it really did seem as if everyone who could be was on the hill.

Jane took a position on the slope, so that everyone could hear what she was saying. It surprised me. She wasn't the sort you'd think would be happy standing in front of so many people, giving orders. She seemed to me to be a quite a timid person really, but this thing was driving her. She looked slightly taller than usual, standing as she was above us, but she still looked small. It was hard to believe she was Alison's mum sometimes. They were close, but physically they were quite different. Alison was much taller, and she had those strange green eyes, and her black hair. I suppose she takes after her father, rather than Jane, whose round face and eyes were framed by a blonde mop. Her hair flapped a bit now as a breeze drifted over us. She pointed here and there, and said how it was that the carving had got into such a state.

Everyone listened while she explained what there was to do, and that we all had to wait for the official from Historic England to oversee the work. There was a loud boo, when she said that.

I got the strangest feeling then. It was nothing to do with what Jane was saying; in fact I think I'd switched off again.

I suddenly felt like I was watching a piece of history; that

I was *in* a piece of history. It was like a biblical scene somehow. Or perhaps something from the Civil War. A group of villagers, standing on the hill, with a common purpose. Something they had to do, getting instructions from their leader. They were about to go and do something; I didn't know what. Something noble perhaps, or something dreadful . . . I wondered how many times there had been gatherings on this hill, through the years. It's the sort of thing that just doesn't happen these days, but Jane was making it happen, right then.

In the end, we started without our official visitor. It was half-past ten, and Jane said we wouldn't get anything done unless we made a start, so we did.

That whole day was one unending, backbreaking slog. The sun was really fierce, even though it was only spring. The site was on a slope, which meant that a lot of the time we were moving up and down the hill, which was exhausting. First we had to pull up the weeds and dig out the brambles. That took most of the morning. There was still no sign of the Historic England official, but we didn't care. They couldn't make us put the weeds back, even if they wanted to. Someone suggested ringing them on a mobile, but it didn't work when they tried. No one volunteered to run down the hill and try from the village. I think we all felt it was our business, this digging on the hill, and if some nosy London organisation wanted to see it happen then they ought to be able to get themselves here on time.

To start with, the mood was quite jolly, but as the morning

wore on, and it seemed as though we were getting nowhere, people started to grumble. Jane got wise to this, and called a lunch break. I hadn't carried any of the food up, but somehow Alison and Jane had got it all there. They must have had help, because there were mountains of rolls and sandwiches. It was a huge picnic, and everyone loosened up again. There was lots of laughter and fooling around.

It was only at lunch, sitting on the hill, looking down at the village, that I noticed something. Despite his rudeness earlier, Robin was sitting with Alison's granddad and some of his other regulars, sharing some beer and a joke or two. I couldn't believe it.

As I sat eating a cheese roll and looking at the village below me, I kept on trying to work out why it was called Crownhill, if it had been there before King Charles. The only thing that made any sense was if it had been called something else before and during the Civil War, and then they had changed the name afterwards, when Charles II came to power.

But that was the one explanation that neither Jane nor Alison had offered. I wondered what the village might have been called. Something to do with the hill, I was sure of that, because it dominated the whole area; such a peculiar, sudden, round bump of a hill.

So we went back to work, and slowly we scoured the crown. I knew Jane and Alison were almost obsessed about it. I didn't know why. Nor did I know why everyone else was doing it. Perhaps they were simply enjoying taking part in a village event. Perhaps my aunt was more persuasive than she looked. And me? I was exorcising some ghosts, sort of. Showing myself that the hill was a nice place to be. I was convincing myself that my dream *had* been only a dream. There could be no witch.

It was very beautiful up there, that day.

And since the fire, I'd had a lot of time to think about things. I wanted to be too busy and too tired to think about stuff like that for a while. Stuff like Kiz.

But I couldn't, and there was something else bothering me. I hadn't been up onto the hill since I came to Crown-hill. Not before the Scouring, I mean. So how did I know what it looked like, before I got there?

Pygine, Russoll, Dunsott, Elemanzer, Pyewackett, Tibb, Ball, Sack-and-Sugar and Grizell Greedi-guts . . . these are the names of their familiars. No Mortal could have invented such names . . .

4

The Old Woman

Noise like a dragon roaring. Windows exploding from their frames, just from the heat. Smoke, thick, black and malevolent; pouring around the door, through the slightest crack. The howl of the smoke alarm that hadn't worked until the fire was already unstoppable. The angry flare of the flames; the only light in an otherwise pitch-dark house.

I woke first, and if I hadn't, then none of us might have got out. I still don't know what woke me, but I got out of bed suddenly, knowing something was wrong. "Mum?" I called, but the noise was too much already. I tried to switch the bedroom light on, but nothing happened. That's when I really started to panic – because of the dark. Desperate for some light, I opened the bedroom door. As I put my hand on the knob, it felt warm, but I didn't realise why until it was too late.

"Mum! Fire!" I screamed, and then my parents' bedroom door opened. There was my dad, still half asleep. Then he saw the flames. The flames leaping up the stairs that lay between us.

Between my parents, and me . . . and my little sister.

I sat on the hill, staring at nothing, trying to squash all the thoughts of that awful night. Trying to make it never have happened, but not managing. Thinking, thinking, thinking and hating it all.

I wanted to get back to the Scouring; sitting around was no good. Too much time to think. I remembered Mrs Chandler, my teacher, telling me I had to get over it. She'd dragged me in to her office for a chat before I took my early break from term.

"Go down to your aunt's and try and forget it, James. It won't do any good to keep on thinking about it all the time."

She waited for me to say something, but I didn't. I merely nodded.

"You have to try and get over it."

I hated sitting there, while she told me how to feel and what to do, but I couldn't face arguing about it, so I just nodded again.

Other people had given me advice too. I'd had plenty of it. I couldn't stand all the fuss.

I wanted to get back to the Scouring. I felt desperate to.

So far, we'd cleared most of the weeds, but grass had overgrown many of the lines of the carving. It would take the rest of the day to uncover them all. And then there was the problem of the chalk itself. It was dirty. A sort of grubby green colour had stained it in a lot of places.

"Bad, isn't it?"

I turned round. There was an elderly lady next to me. She was one of those tiny old ladies you see sometimes. She looked far too frail to be up on the hill, let alone digging and scraping, and she was dressed as though she was about to give a tea party.

"Yes," I said. "Jane says they're going to put fresh chalk into the lines. Then it'll be clean and white again."

"Lovely," said the old lady. "That will look lovely, won't it?"

"Er . . . yes," I said. "But we can't do it today. They'll have to do it later. They need to raise some money to pay for it. And they won't know how much until we see how big the crown really is."

"Lovely," she said again. This threw me slightly.

"It's hard to tell with all the grass that's grown over it, you see."

"Oh, yes," she said, "lovely. Good."

I was relieved to see that work was starting again. I saw Alison getting people back together in groups. When I looked again, the old lady had gone. She must have wandered off somewhere. I picked up a trowel. Then the memory of the fire started to come back into my head. I couldn't stand it. I couldn't *help* it – my brain was doing whatever it wanted. I'd only just managed to stop myself thinking about the fire, and here it came again. But I was wrong; it had been the old lady who'd stopped me thinking about it, but she had gone, and it was coming at me again. The thought of the night our house burned down. Why couldn't I just forget about everything? For a day. For five minutes even. I felt angry now. Angry with myself, with everyone else, as well.

I had lost my gloves somewhere, and without bothering to find them I practically ran, in spite of my aching leg, back to the bed of brambles I'd been working on before lunch.

Within seconds I had the brambles up by the roots, and was on to another patch, nettles this time. I tore into them, until there were none left to pull. My hands were cut from the brambles, and now the nettles stung them too, but I didn't mind. It felt good to throw myself into something. To let go, completely.

I worked until I was exhausted, then sat back, breathing heavily.

Jane came over.

"You've been going at it," she said, "I've been watching you."

"Just thought we needed to get a move on," I lied.

"You're right, but we'll get there."

Then it was onto the carving itself.

It was hard work. Not just exhausting, but complicated, because of the overgrown grass. It had matted over in places, hiding the lines in little tunnels of green. Sometimes you didn't know whether you were looking at the carving, or just a patchy bit of grass on the hillside. All the time people kept stopping to ask Jane whether they should remove a clump or not. She seemed a bit flustered, and more than once I saw her glance down the hill. I guessed she was looking for the woman from Historic England. But there was no sign of her, though it had gone three. Alison was working near me. She was upset. I could tell. She'd been expecting a gang of friends from school to come. Not one of them had. I knew she felt a bit separate from her friends. They all lived in town, and did lots of stuff without her. It was hard – Jane didn't have a car, and the buses were hopeless.

I think she'd known they weren't going to bother coming. But it wasn't just that. I guessed that they still hadn't asked that boy out for her.

She smiled weakly as I came over.

"How are you doing?" she asked.

I pulled a face.

"I'm not sure I know what I'm doing," I said.

"Just between you and me, I'm not sure Mum does either."

I laughed, and Alison laughed too. It seemed to help her be less cross about her friends.

"She looks like she does."

"I know. That's the secret of her success!"

"Is that what she does in the pub, then?" I asked.

"What?"

"Looks like she knows what she's doing."

"No, Robin's too smart for that."

"So why does he put up with her? Being late and so on?"

Alison paused, then smiled.

"They're a bit more than friends, see?"

"Oh, I see," I said.

*

Jane was going around from group to group, advising and encouraging. It was only then that I noticed how few of us there were. I had spent so long staring at the grass in front on my nose that I hadn't realised that quite a lot of people had gone.

I watched as a few more gave up. Jane virtually ran over to them. I couldn't hear what was being said but it was quite clear. She was trying to convince them to stay, and they were saying they'd had enough. They left.

I had some sympathy with them, to be honest. It was a hot day, it was tiring work. My rush of energy after lunch had long since gone. I think I would have packed it in by then, too, but I couldn't. I didn't have a choice.

Jane asked us to turn the dirty chalk over. Just to make it look a bit whiter until the lines were filled with clean, new chalk. But it was hard-going.

More people left.

From our position on the hill, right on top of the chalk carving, we couldn't really tell if all our work was having any effect. Maybe that was why so many people were quitting.

By six we were the only ones left. Jane, Alison and me. Alison's granddad had gone a long time before, when the last of the beer had been drunk.

We worked on, in silence. I could tell Jane was disappointed. I don't know about Alison, but she wasn't saying anything either. She was probably just fed up at having such an embarrassing mother. I bet she was glad none of her friends from school had come, after all.

Finally, we stopped.

"We can't do any more," Jane said, with a sigh.

"I'm sure it'll look much better," Alison said. I think she was trying to convince herself as much as her mum.

"It's so hard to tell, standing on top of it like this. All you can see are a few lines close up."

"It's like being an ant, walking across a huge painting," said Alison. "Of course you can't see anything."

We walked down the hill, not talking. I was fed up, tired out, and I'd had enough of my aunt and her stupid crown.

We got to the back gate to the garden.

"Well," Jane said, "we may as well go and see if we've made any difference."

Alison groaned.

"I'll come," I said quickly, to try and head off a fight.

"Okay, I'm coming too," said Alison.

We walked down the side of the house, along a little path that led straight on to the road. The houses gave out on one side, where the green opened up. As we rounded the corner, we saw something that stopped us dead. Immediately, an uneasy feeling started in me. There were a lot of people, maybe a couple of hundred, standing at the far end of the green.

We walked over. There must have been people from Hesset and Weston, the nearest villages to us, as well as from Crownhill.

As we got closer, we saw they were all looking the same way. Up. At the hill. We still couldn't see why. The old chestnut trees along the edge of the green were blocking our view.

Someone had seen us.

"There she is!" said a voice. The unease in me grew. Instead of friendliness, there was an altogether different tone in the voice. A hostile tone.

And then we saw what we had done.

The thing on the hill, well, it wasn't a crown, that's for sure. What we had uncovered was something else. What ancient lines we had cleared I have no idea. How the thing ever became known as a crown I cannot imagine.

It was *not* a crown.

What we were looking at was a crude picture of a woman. It was primitive, but unmistakable. The face was made by just a few gashes and dots, but the hair was obvious, and even without the hair, you would have known it was a female, because it was naked. The woman was sort of crouching, or squatting, not standing. It was unbelievably shocking to see, as if it had appeared from nowhere.

But we had done it. Jane and Alison, and the villagers, and me.

I was staring so hard at the carving, at the *new* carving, that I hadn't taken much notice of the crowd.

Something was happening. They were backing away from us, but I knew it was Jane they were talking about. People were glancing in our direction, and muttering things to each other.

"The shame!" I heard someone say.

". . . led us on . . ."

". . . she knew it . . ."

That kind of thing, and worse.

The crowd began to disperse, and very soon, we were left alone on the green, the three of us.

We stared at the rude carving, and I wondered what we'd done.

That the girl bears on her right leg The Mark —
placed there by Sathan to seal their evil pact.

That the girl is unable to shed tears, and moreover
refuses to speak of her crimes, even when encouraged
to do so.

That the girl has been heard to speak to her familiar
— the cat known to her as Chub.

That she had the cat, Chub, infect the body and
mind of Richard Sedley, preventing him from
sleeping, hastening his decline and causing his death.

And thus, she is a witch and should be punished
according to the law.

5

Malevolence

"Get that, will you, Jamie," called Jane from the bathroom at the back of the house.

It was the next morning, and the sunny weather had given way to rain.

As soon as I opened the door it was obvious who it was. It had to be the woman from Historic England. She was dressed far too smartly for anyone from the village. There was a shiny car outside the house that was looking fed up at having to drive through the dirty countryside. If these clues weren't enough, the look on her face said it all.

"What on earth have you done to the crown?" she demanded.

"Me?" I said. I didn't even get a chance to say hello. "I . . . it wasn't me."

I had helped to do it, but I didn't think it was fair that I should get all the blame.

"We could prosecute you, you know."

"I think you should speak to my aunt."

"What's going on?" said Jane from behind me. She was

53

still drying her hair with a towel. The woman from Historic England turned her glare on my aunt instead.

"Mrs Graves?" she snapped.

Jane kept cool. I was impressed.

"Jane Graves," she said. "And you must be . . . ?"

"Clare Pitt, Historic England."

She was a bit older than my aunt, with short greyish hair. She looked like she might be miserable most of the time.

And she really was cross.

"Just what exactly do you think you've been doing?" she asked.

"Won't you come inside?"

We were still standing on the doorstep. Jane was glancing at the street. She obviously didn't want anyone to see this little performance. As it was she was not popular in the village. After we'd left the green we'd spent a gloomy evening in the cottage, not talking much. Once or twice Jane said she couldn't see why everyone was so cross with her, why they hated the carving so much. Neither Alison nor I bothered answering. After a while, Alison had gone off to phone one of her friends. She was back very quickly, though, saying they were "all out".

Clare Pitt from Historic England moved into the kitchen, a little grudgingly, I thought. She didn't stop telling Jane that she was in trouble, a lot of trouble, that what she had done was irresponsible, and very possibly illegal.

While this went on, Jane was making some tea. She got some cups and things and was rummaging around in a drawer when Alison came in. Clare Pitt kept up her assault on Jane. Alison looked at me. She pointed a finger secretly at the woman, and mouthed something.

"Is this who I think it is?" or words to that effect.

I nodded. She sat down next to me at the kitchen table and watched the show. The woman from Historic England was working herself up into even more of a state. I think Jane had rattled her by not arguing back.

Alison lent across the table and whispered.

"They ought to call it Hysterical England."

We both started giggling in the way you do when you really shouldn't be. It wasn't even that funny, but then that's never the point.

Finally, Clare Pitt from Hysterical England stopped her abuse. She had noticed Alison and me. She glared, and we stopped sniggering very quickly.

Jane took this chance to stop rummaging in a drawer and say something to our guest.

"Miss Pitt, may I ask you where you were yesterday?"

She turned.

"What on earth has that got to do with anything?"

"Well, you were supposed to be here to oversee the Scouring."

"Nonsense! Today is the day we arranged, and I arrive to find . . ."

Jane was brilliant. She produced a piece of paper from somewhere. I didn't even see where, but it was obvious it was what she had been looking for in the drawer.

"That is your signature at the bottom, isn't it?"

Jane shoved the letter under Clare Pitt's nose. She held it irritatingly close, I think on purpose.

At last, Clare Pitt was silent. She started to go a funny colour. She started to ferret through her handbag.

"No . . . I have the date in my diary. Yes, here we . . . oh."

She went white then. Her face fell, and her mouth closed, slowly.

The kettle finished boiling noisily.

"Some tea, Miss Pitt?" asked Jane, with a concerned look on her face. She was trying not to smile.

After a while we even began to feel a little sorry for Clare Pitt. She was a lot less scary now that her balloon had been popped. "We could never have got everyone together on a Monday, you see," Jane explained. "It had to be done at the weekend."

"I don't know how I could have got the date wrong. The twenty-fifth of April. Sunday the twenty-fifth. I just don't understand how I got it wrong. I never make those sorts of mistakes."

You could tell this was true. You could also tell that it was bothering her, badly.

"My secretary wrote the letter, and I wrote the date in my desk diary there and then . . . it's as though someone's playing a trick on me."

"Never mind, I'm sure they won't be too cross," said Jane.

"Who?"

"Your bosses. At Historic England."

"Oh," she said. She obviously hadn't even thought of that yet. She got even more miserable.

"Never mind. What's done is done, eh?"

Clare Pitt stayed and we had some lunch. We talked about the carving, and how we had only really cleared it, uncovering what was already there. She cheered up a bit, and said she'd like to go and have a proper look, after lunch, of course.

The rain showed no sign of easing as we trudged up the hill. It was hard to believe it had been so warm the day before. We got to the carving and the now calm Miss Pitt had a good nose around.

It was strange to think that for as long as anyone could remember the thing we were standing on had been thought of as a crown. But in the length of a day, it had turned into a huge naked woman. We stood on what was the head of the woman, though there was only a stripe for her nose and that was it. Her womanly features lay elsewhere.

Clare peered at the chalk and the ground next to it, nearly on her knees despite the muddy soil. She seemed satisfied, in fact, she seemed quite pleased. Almost excited. It was getting colder, and the rain was getting harder. We came down off the hill, and despite the rain, Clare Pitt from Historic England was quite jolly.

We couldn't be sure at the time, but it seemed that she had half-expected something like this to happen herself. She said she had some papers and things to show us when we got back to the cottage. She was quite chatty.

"Beautiful part of the world this, isn't it?"

Alison and I looked at each other. The day before had

been lovely, but this was a cold, grey drizzling April afternoon. We were looking forward to getting in out of the nasty weather.

"Yes, yes," she went on, "and so many local traditions."

"You mean festivals, and things like that?" Jane asked. I think she was finding it hard to cope with the complete change in Clare's character since the onslaught we'd had on her arrival.

"Well, yes, But other things too. For instance, your gateposts. No, the ones at the front. Those markings on it are most unusual."

Jane stopped. Alison groaned, again. I think she was expecting a phone call from Rebecca, one of her friends, and wanted to get back in case. Anyway, we were so nearly at the house, and it was raining harder now than before.

Jane wasn't interested in the weather though.

"There aren't any markings on my gates," she said.

"No, no, on the posts."

"There are none there either."

"Oh yes, there are. I saw them this morning, quite clearly. You know what they are, don't you?"

"Show me," said Jane, suspiciously.

Clare Pitt marched us around to the front of the cottage. She was right; there was a series of lines cut into the wooden gateposts. They were sort of crossed, at diagonals to each other.

"There you are," said Miss Pitt. She was pleased with herself. Jane said nothing.

"So what are they then?" I asked. I can't stand it when people are being deliberately mysterious.

"Witch marks," she said.

Alison said, "Pardon?"

"Those are quite distinctive markings. They appear first in the seventeenth century, as far as we know, but they were probably being made long before that date. They are marks made by people to ward against witches and witch-craft. To guard against evil as it were. They are supposed to prevent a witch from passing through."

She stopped.

"How creepy," Alison said.

"But that's odd," Miss Pitt continued.

"What?" I said.

"Well, now that I look at them closely, you can see they're not old at all. See how the wood is lighter in colour in the scratches. And the edges of the cuts are still sharp. As if they were made yesterday."

"Or even last night," Alison said grimly.

It was true. These ancient marks to protect against witches were obviously new. Possibly just a few hours old.

"Let's go inside, I'm freezing," I said.

We did, but Jane hovered for a moment, staring silently at the lines carved into her gateposts. She hesitated a moment longer; she seemed reluctant to walk through the gates, but at last, she came in too.

Despite the fact that it was late April, and not yet six, it was very dark in the house. We went into the tiny, low-ceilinged sitting room. We sat, and thought.

Clare Pitt prattled on about this and that to do with the hill carving, mostly various theories about when it was made. Jane wasn't taking much notice. It was obvious she was thinking about the scratches on her gateposts, but she nodded and hummed at the right places. Clare said something about some papers to do with the village, that she had brought to show us, but Jane said she would light a fire first. She did, and I watched her do it.

I watched Jane grab some old newspapers from the bucket by the hearth. She screwed them up into long fingers and then wound them around to make balls the size of her fist.

I watched her place the newspaper balls in the grate.

Her hand moved to the mantelpiece. I was dimly aware of Clare and Alison making awkward conversation on the far side of the room, but my eyes were glued to what Jane was doing.

Her fingers had reached the mantelpiece, but then she muttered something I didn't hear, and her hand moved away from the small thing that it had been going to find. I struggled to remember what it would be she was looking for. One stick after another, until finally she had made a little stack over the paper, like a tiny wooden wigwam.

I *watched* her do it. I watched her.

Then she stood up, and her hand moved out again, up towards the mantelpiece, her fingers feeling for something. They knew what she was trying to find; why didn't I? Her hand stopped and the fingers closed around the small box. It rattled slightly as she knelt down in front of the hearth.

I watched, but I couldn't breathe.

Holding the small yellow box in her left hand, she pointed her right index finger at its end. Then she moved box against finger, and the tiny cardboard drawer slid out of the other end.

I remembered. I opened my mouth, but it was too late.

She was already taking the tiny but powerful piece of wood from inside. Inside the head of that little bit of wood there was danger, but she didn't seem to know, and I . . . I tried to tell her, but I wasn't able to.

Then she struck the match.

I saw in slow motion how the pink head slid jerkily across the rough brown bumps on the side of the match-box. Inside that pink head was a dangerous chemical. A chemical that held the power of a frightening reaction.

As the thing slipped and skipped over each brown bump on the side of the box, a little spark jumped away from the head of the match. Any one of them could set the whole thing off, and then one of them did.

The match exploded into fire, and then suddenly there was fire everywhere. The fire filled the entire room in a second. I couldn't see Jane or Alison or anything, just walls of fire all around me. I was too scared to wonder how the fire had spread from the match to the whole room, but it had. In an instant it had surrounded me; a huge roaring wall of fire, and thick, thick, choking, black smoke.

I was cut off, and there was no escape.

The fire came closer, onto my shoes, and then my hands, and then my hair. I felt my eyes burn, and I knew that somewhere at the other end of my house was my family.

My mum and dad, and little Kiz, I couldn't get to them. And they couldn't get to me.

The witch was found at her lair on the hill where she was consulting with her familiar, the cat named Chub. It was clear from the leaves of herbs around about that they were preparing some more injurious mischief to inflict upon one person or another.

The witch struggled as she was taken, but her familiar escaped, clearly in a magical fashion.

The witch kicked violently as she was placed in a cell. Some hours later she was presented to the judges of the court for the first time.

She made no response to any question.

6

The Naming of Things

"Your mum's on the phone," said Alison from the doorway.

I looked at Jane. She looked at the doctor. A little woman of about forty, I guess, and obviously a friend of Jane's.

"I've finished," she said, "for now." She packed her doctor things away. She smiled at Jane.

"I'll look in, tomorrow. Day after maybe. But ring me if you need to."

"Thanks, Susan."

The doctor left.

Alison coughed.

"Well?"

"You can go and talk to your mum now, Jamie," said Jane.

I hesitated.

"Can you tell her I'm still asleep?" I said quietly.

"Jamie . . .!" began Alison, but Jane interrupted her.

"I'll go," she said. "I think that's best for now."

"Thank you," I said.

Jane went downstairs and Alison watched her go.

Then we were alone. Just like we had been after the dream had hit me.

"Don't you want to speak to your mum?"

"I don't know," I said.

"Because . . . ?"

Because it's none of your business, I thought.

I shrugged.

"I wish your mum hadn't told her about it," I said, "me fainting."

"You did a little bit more than faint, Jamie," said Alison.

I began to protest.

"You know she had to tell your mum. Things like that are important."

"Yes, but now she'll try and make me come home."

"I thought you wanted to go home."

How did she know that? I wasn't sure of it myself any more.

"I do. I did."

I wanted to find out what this place was doing to me. The dream was no ordinary dream. And the chalk on my feet. I couldn't just run away and forget it all. Supposing it came with me? Supposing *she* came with me.

Alison tried again.

"If you don't talk to her, she's definitely going to insist that you go home."

I knew I didn't want to talk to my mum, but I didn't know why. And Alison insisting that I should made it worse. Just because she and *her* mother talked about things didn't mean I had to with mine.

66

"Who knows," I said. "She wanted to send me here in the first place. I didn't want to come."

"Maybe we didn't want you to come either," said Alison, nastily.

There was a pause.

"I don't mean it like that," I said.

"I know," said Alison, quickly. "Sorry."

"I don't see why I couldn't have stayed and helped. Better than being down here and thinking about . . ."

"The fire?" asked Alison.

I looked away. But nodded.

"It must have been dreadful," said Alison.

I ignored her. She tried again.

"What was it like?"

I ignored her even harder.

"Sorry," she said.

I snapped.

"It was like your house burning down in the middle of the night, okay?"

She said nothing.

"Okay?" I yelled.

She left the room. I think I fell asleep again not long after that.

Jane came to see me later, with some soup on a tray. By the fading light outside I guessed that it was late in the afternoon. She put the tray next to my bed, on the little table. I watched her do it.

"Alison says sorry."

"No problem," I said. "I'm sorry too."

For everything, I thought.

"You know, James, if you ever feel like talking about it . . ."

I nodded.

". . . what happened. With your parents and . . ."

She stopped.

"Kiz," I said. There. Now I'd said her name.

She put her hand on mine.

"So, what did Mum say?" I asked, to change the subject.

"Well, she's very worried about you. Obviously. She's going to ring back later tonight, or tomorrow if you're asleep again. Try and talk to her if you can. If only to stop her worrying."

I pulled a face.

She smiled.

"Okay."

"When you feel up to it, I'll tell you what Clare Pitt's been telling us about the history of the village."

"Tell me now," I said. "Please."

"Well, if you want to come downstairs, you can have a look at the papers she's left behind for us."

Jane and Alison had been browsing through the papers in the sitting room. I hesitated in the doorway.

"Oh, Jamie," said Jane, "I should have thought. Do you want to sit in the kitchen?"

"No." I said, "I'll be all right."

I noticed that Jane had either never lit the fire or had let it go out. She had realised that it might not be a good idea for me to see a fire again so soon, but she hadn't thought that the room itself might still scare me.

It didn't scare me, but I found it very confusing. Yesterday, I had stood pretty much right where I was now and yelled my head off, convinced that I was back in my house, my *real* home, with the walls dripping flame around me. I stared at the fireplace now, in Jane's cottage, but there wasn't even the beginning of fear in me. I didn't understand that.

"Come and sit here," said Alison, nodding at the seat next to her on the sofa. I did. She seemed calm and friendly now, and it rubbed off on me.

"What's that then?" I asked, pointing at the paper Alison was reading.

The first thing Clare had told Alison and Jane was that the village used to be called something else.

It seemed I was right. Just as I'd worked out on the hill during the Scouring – the village had to have been called something different before the Civil War, and then they changed the name as a sign of loyalty to King Charles when he came back to power.

But I was wrong.

"Yes," said Jane, "it used to be called Cronhill. See?"

She waved a photocopy of an old document at me. I couldn't read it, but it didn't matter.

"Is that just an old spelling, then?" I asked, disappointed. If it was, then my idea didn't help make any sense of it at all.

"I suppose so," said Jane.

"When was it called that?"

"She's not sure," Alison said. She meant Clare Pitt. "The only record of it being called that is from 1583. There's nothing after that until some point in the seventeenth century. Then it's good old Crownhill."

I looked at the photocopy in more detail. If you really concentrated you could just about understand the writing. The letters were small and cramped up against each other, and the language was strange. After a few lines I felt like giving up. I could read something about someone's property in the village of Cronhill being sold to someone else. Clare had underlined the name in red pen to show us. I read on a bit. The property was The Red Barn – the yellow barn on the green.

"Look," I said, "it's about The Red Barn."

Alison and Jane peered at the paper.

"Oh, yes."

"Stupid, isn't it?" I said.

"What?" asked Jane.

"Why it's called the Red Barn when it's yellow."

"Perhaps it used to be red," said Alison, "and they got bored and painted it yellow, but the name stuck."

That got me thinking about the name of the village again. A thought was trying to get out of my head, but Jane spoke and it vanished.

"That's not why it's called The Red Barn," she said. She looked at Alison. "Don't you know the story?"

"Nope," said Alison blankly.

"How extraordinary," said her mother. She sighed. "I suppose I didn't tell you when you were younger, because,

70

well, and then it's just not the sort of thing you talk about."

"So!" asked Alison impatiently.

Jane looked at me, as if she was trying to decide something.

"It's got nothing to do with the colour," she said slowly. "It's because of what happened there. A very, very long time ago. A man, someone not very wealthy, was in love with the Lord of the Manor's daughter. And she was in love with him. So they decided to run away together. They arranged to meet in a barn that belonged to the girl's father, but instead of running away, the man murdered the girl, and buried her under the earth in the barn. Then he hanged himself from a beam way up above where the girl's body lay. They found her because her blood stained the soil. That's why it's called The Red Barn."

Alison and I sat staring open-mouthed at this gruesome story.

"Sorry, dears, but you did ask. Anyway, it's most probably not true, and it did happen a very long time ago. Bad things happen all the time, don't they."

To me, the fact that it happened along time ago didn't make much difference. I felt tired again, but really didn't want to sleep after that gem of a story.

"Not the first time there's been something like that in Crownhill, is it," said Alison.

"What do you mean?" I asked.

Alison shrugged, and said nothing.

Jane was silent for a moment too, as if weighing

something up. She glanced at Alison, then answered my question.

"She means the deaths," said Jane. "Over the years there's always been inexplicable deaths in the village. Not very often. Hasn't been one since the 1940s, they reckon."

"That's not true!" Alison said. "What about Mr Palmer last year?"

"Just because they couldn't find an exact cause of death doesn't mean . . ."

"It's no different from the others, though, is it?"

Jane ignored her daughter, and turned to me again.

"Anyway. For as long as anyone can remember, people have been found dead in their beds. Just normal people. No real pattern to it. Young, old, male, female. Go to bed one night and never wake up in the morning. It's become a bit of a joke these days. But *if* it happened again, people wouldn't find it very funny."

She looked at Alison sharply.

"And no one knows why at all?"

Jane shook her head.

Then she did something weird. She pointed at the piles of photocopied records. "If you find anything about something like that in that lot, let me know, will you?"

I started pushing through some of the other copies of old documents that related to the village. Jane went out to make some tea, and Alison followed her. The sound of their voices drifted in to the sitting room from the kitchen. They seemed to be arguing again, and I heard my name mentioned more than once. I couldn't make much of it out, but then I heard a few clear sentences.

"We have to tell the others," said Alison.

"Not yet. Anyway there's nothing to tell."

"Try telling Jamie that."

Then they must have realised the kitchen door was ajar, because they stopped talking altogether. I went on reading the photocopied sheets in front of me, though I was thinking more about what Jane and Alison had been talking about. Then I saw a word that made me forget all that. I'd been looking at some papers from the seventeenth century. I knew because there were modern catalogue dates along the top of each photocopied sheet. For a while I'd stared at them without making any sense of anything, but I'd seen that one word.

Witchcraft. I held my breath for a long time.

In spite of the fact that the paper I was holding was a photocopy of a very smudged, old and badly written document, that one word jumped out at me, like Robin's words had on Sunday morning at the pub.

Witchcraft. The dream suddenly came bursting back into my head. The witch, chasing me. My hands started to shake, but I read desperately now, pulling the lamp right over to the sofa so I see more clearly. I lost my place for a moment while I did this, but I was not mistaken; there it was again.

I read.

A most curious and foul case of witchcraft has this day been reported as occurring during the suspension of the assizes during the still remembered strife between the King and Parliament.

A young woman of sixteen years was brought before the law, having been accused of using the power of evil spirits to injure certain animals belonging to persons known to her, to prevent the milk of certain persons from turning into butter, and to injure until dead a youth known as Richard Sedley, who had formerly announced her to be a witch.

This all occurring some fifteen years ago in the village of Crownhill in the county of Somerset, a village long troubled by the curse of witchcraft, in the year of Our Lord 1658.

7

The Fear is Coming

A strange, dark, black thing. Rotting coarse cloth, grimy and smelly, stained with unknown foul marks. The thick cloth is right under my nose. I can smell its rank decaying fibres. It is the most repulsive thing I have ever seen. It is *so* horrible and disgusting that perversely I am tempted to reach out and touch it, but my lips quiver at the thought, and I am nearly sick. The black lump of cloth, which is right in front of my face, moves, a slight twitch, and then is still.

On top, slightly askew, there is something else, even more disgusting than the rotten sacking it is sitting on. I lean closer, to get a better look. It is so dark, I cannot see properly. I lean closer, and wait for my eyes to really see.

Long, straggly wisps. Thick, matted clumps. A revolting smell. I lean back again slightly, trying not to puke. It passes. I hold my breath and lean in again so that my eyes are just a couple of inches from the thing. I realise what I am looking at. It is . . . wool? No. It is hair, like a horse's tail, perhaps. A tail of a horse that hasn't been cared for and is covered in filth. But then I see something else. There are bare patches between some of the matted lumps of hair. In these bare patches I can see something so white it is evil.

And then it moves. Not just a twitch this time, but a shudder. The ball of hair in front of my face rolls, twisting awkwardly on the rotting cloth.

I am looking into the face of the witch.

I throw up and scream all at the same time, trying to push myself backwards and failing. The floor of the foul pit I am in is covered in a stinking mess of putrefying slime and my hands just wallow in it.

The witch opens her slit-mouth and a sound comes out. A really frightening sound. She is laughing.

She gets up from the stinking mattress bed where she has been lying and with a grunt and a fart she stands up on uneven legs. I catch a glimpse of her legs through the decaying sack-dress as she does so. I cannot help but look, but this is not like stealing a glimpse at the thighs of one of the classy girls at school. The legs I see are white, as white as leprosy, withered and thin and blotchy and covered in sores, and I am sick again, though I have nothing left in me to puke with.

For a moment, though, my luck changes, and just as she is about to touch me with one of her stringy claw-hands, my feet find something solid to push against.

With one push, I am back in bed. But I am not safe, because just like the last time, she knows where I am. Now that she knows, I cannot escape.

78

Somehow, from where I am trapped in my bed, I can see out of the window, across the curve of the hill and down into the foul pit where she lives. She looks up at me, and laughs. With a spring of her hideous legs she is out of the hole and straight away she starts hobbling for me again. The fact that I have seen this unnerving walk once before doesn't make it any less scary this time. In fact, it is worse. How fast she moves with that stupid crippled run.

I try to get out of bed, to go for help, but I cannot even move my toes. I can't turn my head. I realise that I can't even blink, let alone shut my eyes. So I have to watch as she heads out of her burrow and comes for me. Over and along the hill. Then she disappears out of sight, heading down the hill. Now I cannot see her, it's worse still. Frantically I try and work out exactly where she will have got to, and just as I reckon she's at the bottom of the hill, her face is at my window, evil and white.

I try to scream.

Her fingers touch the window glass.

With relief, I see that the latch is down. But the witch wags a nasty finger, and the window starts to slide open.

I wake up, silently howling at the dark room.

The witch was brought before the judges for a second time, but still she displayed no remorse for what she had done, nor would she utter a single word. This despite her being watched and kept awake for eighteen straight hours previous to this second trial.

The witch was taken down from the court, to be returned to her cell. As she did so, the crowd watching her made several shouts at her. These she ignored, until one John Sedley, brother of the dead Richard, shouted to her saying that he had her cat and would do harm to it.

At this the witch made the first show of her devilment and cursed John Sedley, then collapsed into a state of sorcerous sleep.

And this is the curse, as I was told it: "A loaf in my lap, a penny in my purse, I am ever better, And thou art ever worse."

8

The Trial

I didn't tell anyone about the second dream. Not then, anyway. I had started to suspect that Alison and Jane knew more than they were telling me about what was going on. I didn't think there was anyone else I could tell.

It took me a long time to shake it off, though. Whenever I closed my eyes, I could see her white face leering at me, as if she was just a few inches away. There was a nasty taste in my mouth, like the smell of her foul breath. I could feel myself starting to lose control. I made a real effort to push her out of my mind, but it was hard. It was as if she was all around me now, even in the daylight. Then I thought of something I could do. I wanted to talk to Clare Pitt. But it was Susan, the doctor, I saw next.

In fact, I didn't see her at all, I only heard her. I was still in bed. I couldn't face more inquisitions, so when I heard Jane let Susan in, I pretended to still be asleep. I heard them coming up the stairs.

I heard Jane say, "I don't know. I'll see if he's awake yet."

"Well, it's late, but if he's sleeping that's the best thing for him."

I shut my eyes as I saw the door start to open. It creaked slightly, then shut again. Then I heard Jane whispering outside again.

"Yes, he is," she said.

"Good," said Susan. "Well, I'll come back."

"Susan, there was one other thing."

"Yes?"

"You saw Mr Palmer, didn't you? Before he died?"

There was a pause.

"Yes. Why?"

"I just wondered."

"Jane, you're my friend. You know that. But you know I can't talk about other cases."

Their voices went down the stairs, and I could hear no more.

Mr Palmer. I'd heard that name before. I remembered. He was the man who'd died strangely last year. With no explanation.

Clare had promised to come back soon after breakfast, and she did.

"When was this written?" I asked. I showed her the paper I'd been reading the day before.

She smiled.

"Finding the local history interesting, James?"

I ignored this, but put the question another way.

"Where does it come from?"

She took the paper from me. I knew she didn't really

know what to make of me. I supposed Jane had told her why I was living there and so on, and as for hallucinating that fire in the sitting room . . . I don't know what she thought about that.

"We're not entirely sure, but it comes from a book of records kept by a local squire in the early part of the eighteenth century. This part here, where it mentions the '*strife between King and Parliament*', that's the Civil War. We think the man who wrote this was writing at least ten years after that."

"Have you read all this?" I asked.

"No, only bits, I got one of my people to dig out anything on the area that we had. You never know what might be relevant to the hill carving, you see?"

How true, I thought.

"But have you read all about this witchcraft trial?"

"Yes, a little. Fascinating, isn't it?"

That wasn't the word I'd have used. Horrific. Scary. Something like that, maybe. The sheets weren't in order; it wasn't like reading a book from one end to the other. There were bits missing, and whoever had put the collection together had only put in the bits they thought were relevant. But the bits I'd found so far told of a girl, I hadn't found out what her name was, being tried for witchcraft in the village. There was a lot I didn't understand.

"What does this mean?" I pointed at a particular word.

"Assizes? Assizes were the law courts. You have to remember that there wasn't the same transport then that there is now. It was much harder for people to get to places, the big towns and so on. So there were sessions of law, held in one place at one time, when all the crimes from the previous few months would be brought to court."

"But why does it say 'suspension of the assizes' then?"

"The piece you're looking at – about this witch trial – that's from the Civil War. The assizes stopped altogether then."

"So what happened instead?"

"Nothing very organised. Things happened on a more local level – unofficial courts in smaller towns and villages. They didn't really have the authority, but there was no one to stop them. And it was better than complete anarchy, though that's often how things ended up."

I looked at Clare.

"How do you mean?"

"Well, the Civil War, and the period from then until the King was restored, coincided with the height of the witch-craze."

"Witch-craze?"

"It was a bad time. Things were out of control. Some men started calling themselves Witch-finders, though they had no authority to. The most famous was called Matthew Hopkin; he lived in East Anglia. But there were others too, some around here. They went around accusing anyone they thought was a witch. Most often old women, but young ones too sometimes. Men occasionally. Once you had been accused, there was very little you could do to prove your innocence. Whole villages could turn into the judge and jury. Pick on someone who was unpopular, or foreign, or just different. Mob rule. Mob executions."

Clare's words started my heart beating hard. I felt . . .

afraid. Something popped into my head. I don't know where it came from. Not a thought. I mean, not just a thought. It was much more *powerful*. It was a girl, screaming, because she . . . all around her . . . flames. I could almost see it, right in front of my open eyes. I shook my head, and looked at Clare.

"They . . . *burnt* them," I said, quietly.

Clare looked at me.

"No, actually. They burnt witches in Scotland. They burnt witches in the rest of Europe. But we preferred to hang them, here."

She smiled.

"Really? But I always thought they were burnt."

"So do most people, but there it is. A common piece of popular fiction. There are maybe one or two cases in England where the victims were burnt. Maybe."

I wasn't convinced, but she was the expert. I couldn't push the picture of the girl from my head, though. Not completely. There was something about fire, about fire and her, I was convinced.

"So what about this girl, then?

"What about her?"

"Well, this curse she uses. Doesn't that show she was a witch? Or at least thought she was?"

I showed Clare the extract from the trial.

"No, I don't think so. It's not a very strong curse, is it? I would think it's probably just a folk saying, something anyone might say."

"But look . . ." I began, but Jane came in.

"Right then!" she said. "Back up the hill?"

"Lovely," said Clare. They'd been getting on better and better since their bad start. Now it was as if they were old school friends. I couldn't stand it.

"Coming, Jamie?" asked Jane.

"No, I wanted to ask Clare something."

But neither of them was listening to me.

"Yes, you stay here," said Clare. "Get some rest. See you at lunch time."

They left, discussing the old chalk woman on the hill. Don't ask me why, but it was only then that I realised the connection. It was obvious. So obvious that I think my mind must have been denying it, stopping it from coming out.

An old woman on the hill, an old woman in my dream.

A witch.

Suddenly there were witches everywhere. A ancient one in my dreams, and a young girl in the notes I'd been reading. I didn't understand. I thought again about fire, and went cold.

I felt very alone. I never wanted to dream again. But that would mean never sleeping again.

I went back to reading through some of the extracts, and it was then that I came across the link. When I found it, or rather them, because there were two bits that made my heart race when I read them, I knew the connection was complete. Unavoidable. Inevitable.

I read through the two bits again and again. They were very short, but they made all the difference. They took away all doubt.

I went to find Alison.

"You awake?"

I knocked on Alison's door again. It was nearly lunch-time, but Alison had been keeping to strict holiday hours since the Scouring.

"Alison?"

"Mmm?"

"Can I come in?"

"Mmm."

I went in. I wanted to talk to someone, and I wanted to know some things. I wanted to hold onto what I'd just found out for a little while, until I found out what it was that Alison and Jane were keeping from me.

I knew Alison would probably not tell me, but I had a trick up my sleeve. How was I to know it would backfire on me so badly?

"Jane's told me," I said, shrugging my shoulders, and sighing as if I understood everything.

Alison sat bolt upright.

"She *what*?"

I kept my nerve. I think the fact that she had been half asleep helped.

"Yes," I said, "About telling the others, and about my dream."

She looked around the room.

"I don't believe it . . ." She shook her head. "How could she . . . and she's supposed to be our . . ."

I was desperate for her to finish that sentence, but she was so shocked, and I mean really shocked, that she just tailed off. As far as she was concerned I knew it all anyway. Whatever "it" was.

"That's so unlike her. She's always telling us how important it is to keep quiet, and then to tell you about the dream . . ."

"Well, maybe she thinks it doesn't matter, since it's already happened."

Alison looked at me sharply. I was treading on thin ice; I couldn't afford to say something that would give the game away.

"Yes, but there's a difference between having a bad nightmare, and what having *the dream* means. She shouldn't have told you."

Alison sat up in bed and pushed a hand through her long black hair. I didn't say anything – I couldn't think of anything that was safe to say. Fortunately, or as it turned out, unfortunately, she went on.

"Still, at least you've only had it the once; there's hope. It's the third time that really matters, but then I suppose she told you all that too?"

I nodded automatically. She was so cross with her mother that it all came spilling out. Well, nearly all.

She swung her legs out of bed and pulled her jeans on. She shoved a jumper on over her T-shirt, and started to make noises about having it out with Jane. I knew I'd get found out, but by then, I didn't care.

She stopped for a moment and put a hand on my shoulder.

"Don't worry, Jamie. You'll be all right. I expect it's gone away. It's not like you've had it twice even, is it?"

I shook my head. She didn't know I was lying.

"Twice would be bad, but it's the third one . . ."

"The third one?" I asked quietly, but she was gone.

I sat on her bed, staring into space.

Then did the squire visit the witch, but she would say nothing. Then did the priest visit the witch, but she said nothing still. Then did the witch's mother visit the witch, but she merely stared at her own kind.

Then did one Simon Sexton come to the cell, and he spoke with the priest about certain evil drawings and symbols that the girl had drawn on the walls of her mother's cottage.

The priest questioned the witch about these marks, accusing her of trying to awaken the old woman, but again the witch would say nothing.

Then the witch slept again, clearly making more evil spells in the realm of her sleep.

9

The Making of a Witch

One dream. Two dreams.

There would be a third; I knew that now. Unfortunately, I didn't know when it would come. From the way Alison had talked about it I knew it would be bad. I sat on Alison's bed for what seemed like a long time. Then I decided I had to find out the rest of the truth. I ran out of the bedroom, and leapt down the stairs, which thumped under my weight.

Alison would have followed Jane and Clare up the hill, so I left by the back door to the kitchen, but as I burst through it I saw a group of three figures crouching on the path, *inside* Jane's garden. The moment they saw me, they were up and running. They practically pulled the old gate off its rusty hinges, and fled. This only took a second or two, and then they were gone, but in that time I saw three children – a girl and two boys, I think. I hardly saw one of them. I knew from the way they reacted that this was not just a bit of ordinary trespassing, the sort kids do all the time. They were shocked at seeing me come through the door – more than that – they were terrified.

Also, I knew from the way they'd been crouching over the path that they'd been doing something, and it didn't take long to find out what. When I saw what they'd done, though, it didn't make much sense.

In the mud, just inside the back gate, were several footprints. None of them were small enough to belong to the trespassers. In fact, I recognised Jane's footprints from the soft walking boots she wore everywhere.

Sticking out of these footprints was a row of thorns. In some of the prints there was just a single huge thorn, but in others there was a short piece of hawthorn with several spikes sticking into the mud.

It was inexplicably creepy.

"Is your aunt in?" said a voice.

I looked up into the huge face of Robin Hunt. He didn't seem angry this time, but even so I felt intimidated.

I stared at him, unable to answer his simple question. Then I saw that he was looking at the thorns in the mud. I looked at them again.

"Just what are you doing there then?" he asked, gruffly.

"No . . ." I said, "no, it wasn't me. I just found them. Just a second ago. It was some kids, they ran off round the back of the house."

"I saw them," he said, calming down. I was relieved that he believed me.

"Where's Jane then?" he asked again. "Up the hill?"

I nodded.

"You'd better come," he added.

96

He started to go.

"What about these?" I stammered. "Shall I . . . ?"

"No. Leave them. Up the hill."

Once more I climbed up onto that hill, so full of nasty stuff lurking. For a big man, Robin moved fast up the steep path that led to the carving. Here and there the chalk underneath the soil poked through, a disgusting evil dirty white colour; it reminded me of something I wanted to forget about. Suddenly I didn't want to go on. We were getting near the carving.

"Robin." I panted behind him as he headed up onto the old witch.

"Robin!"

He didn't hear me. I stopped, trying to decide whether to go after him or go back, but my mind was made up for me, because coming in the other direction were Alison and Jane. I couldn't see Clare.

I waited and watched as they met Robin. There was a moment's discussion and then they headed for me.

"You sneaky little . . ."

"That's enough, Alison!" Jane interrupted.

But Alison wasn't finished. She was really cross.

"You must think I'm pretty stupid."

"Well you fell for it, didn't you?" I said, nastily. I didn't see why I should be in trouble just for trying to find out what was happening to me.

"You've no idea what you're playing at!"

"Well, perhaps you'd like to tell me! Then I wouldn't have to be sneaky, would I?"

"That's enough!" said Jane.

"No it isn't."

"Alison stop it!"

This was from Robin, and it worked.

There was a pause.

"Where's Clare?" I asked.

"What . . . oh, up on the carving, still," said Jane.

"What's she doing?"

"Measuring, recording," said Jane, vaguely.

"Doesn't she want any help?" I asked.

Alison snorted.

"Of course she needs help, but Mum suddenly got it into her head to leave."

Jane shrugged her shoulders.

"I just think I, we, need to come off the hill," she said, defensively.

Robin looked at Jane strangely. It wasn't a look that anyone else was meant to see.

"Why?" I asked.

Jane shrugged again.

"I don't know," she said.

Robin showed them the thorns in the footprints.

"Whose footprints are those?" he asked.

"Mine," said Jane quietly.

"Who did it?" asked Alison.

Robin looked at me.

"You . . . ?" began Alison.

"No!" I said. "He means I saw who did it."

"Well?"

"Some kids," I said. "Three of them. Younger than me."

"Describe them," Alison said. She was still cross with me, and seemed to be holding me responsible for everything.

"I didn't really see, they ran off as . . ."

"It doesn't matter," said Jane. "It doesn't matter whose children they were. What matters is that anyone would do it."

Yet again, I had the feeling that everyone knew what was going on except me, but just as I was about to demand some answers, Alison saw Clare coming back.

"Quick! Get rid of it," said Jane, "we don't want her going on about this too."

With his huge feet, Robin swept the thorns and sticks into the hedge by the path. Jane turned to Clare.

"How are you getting on?" she smiled, asked, smiling?

"Fine," said the now happy Historic England official. "Any chance of some lunch?"

"On me," said Robin, "at the pub."

He ushered Clare away.

"Thanks," Jane mouthed to him as they went.

"She's getting a bit close to the truth," Jane said as we sat down to our own lunch.

"Shame I'm not," I said.

Alison grunted.

"No!" I said. "I've had enough. You both know more than you're telling me. Why can't you be honest? Why all the secrecy?"

"Jamie . . ." began Jane.

"We don't have to tell him anything," said Alison. "It's none of his business. We didn't ask him to come down here."

"And I didn't ask for my house to burn down!" I shouted. I stopped. I was cross but I was getting fed up with arguments. I couldn't take any more. Any more trouble. After the fire, now this.

Jane took the chance to speak. Calmly.

"If you two could stop shouting at each other for a little while . . . No Alison, it was you who told me in the first place. He had the dream, didn't he? None of us have ever had it, so why Jamie? It *is* important. Jamie's got a right to know."

Alison nodded.

"I know that. *I* told *you*." She was trying to save face.

"So?" I asked.

Jane looked at me.

"Alison, and Robin, and I. And a lot, well, *some* of the other villagers. We have a sort of organisation. It's a sort of . . . *society* . . . and we've been trying to find out about the carving on the hill for a long time."

I was totally lost at this point. But she went on, and it started to dawn on me what she was saying, though she was picking her words very carefully, and spoke slowly.

"We thought there might be something up there. On the hill, I mean. Something other than a crown. So we set about trying to find out about it."

"So you knew it was really a woman up there?"

100

"No. Not really. We guessed it might be something like that."

"But it doesn't make sense, the fact that we uncovered the shape of a woman underneath the soil so easily, it can't have been covered up for very long or we'd never have found it."

"So?" said Alison.

"Well, if it's not that old, then someone would remember it, or there'd be photos or even just drawings of it."

Jane shrugged her shoulders.

"I know, it's been bothering me too. But all the records we've been able to find out about it call it 'the crown', and there were even a couple of official archaeological digs here in the 1920s, and yet everyone thought it was a crown. It looked nothing like a crown, it's true, but no one thought it was anything *else*."

"So how did we find it so easily then? After all this time?"

Jane didn't answer. I looked at Alison, who said nothing for a while.

"I think it was waiting."

"To be found?"

She shrugged, just the same gesture as her mother.

There was a silence, in which we each dwelled on our own odd thoughts.

"So what were those kids doing? The thorns?"

"They think we're witches," said Jane, bluntly.

"Mum!"

"Well he might as well know what they think of us."

"It's okay," I said, "I don't think you're witches."

I smiled, to show it was a joke. I didn't get much of a response.

"There's been a lot of resistance in the village to what we've been doing. It was hard to get so many people to go to the Scouring, and then it turned their stupid crown into a giant naked woman."

"And they think you're devil-worshippers because of that?"

"People can be very superstitious," said Jane.

That wasn't really an answer, but I let it go.

"It's not just that, though, is it. Mum," Alison said.

Jane sighed.

"No," she said. "no, it isn't."

She looked at me.

"It's because we're outsiders."

"Outsiders?"

"Newcomers to the village."

"But you grew up here, didn't you?"

"Near here. And my father lives here, but Alison and I moved away. When we went to Germany. We don't really belong in the village. That's what the *real* villagers say. Or some of them anyway."

"But that's silly. You've been back here for three years, haven't you?"

"Yes. But that's what it can be like in the country. Someone came up to me the other day, and do you know what she said? She said, don't worry, I'm a newcomer too, I've only been here twelve years."

"But why should it make any difference?"

"It might not, but the trouble is that it's mostly newcomers like us who are interested in the carving, and what it means. The real locals, who have grown up with it, they mostly aren't interested or think it should be left alone. There's only a couple, like Robin, who want to help. And no one says anything bad about Robin because he owns the pub."

"So," I said, "your group. Your group is mostly made up of people new to the village? And the rest of the village thinks you're meddling with the devil!"

"Well, that's putting it a bit simply," said Jane, "but yes. There's a lot of gossip and rumours spread about the village. About what we're doing."

"In fact," said Alison, "witches don't even *believe* in the devil." I must have looked doubtful.

"The devil, Satan, *whatever*, belongs in the Christian religion. He's nothing to do with witchcraft."

"But what about all that stuff about pacts with the devil? Like in the trial of the girl in the old papers?"

"What happened then," Alison said, "during the witch hunts, has got very little to do with witchcraft. The idea that witches worship the devil was put about by the church, to try and turn people against the old pagan religions. And you can be sure that most of those poor women executed as witches were innocent. They might have been herbalists, or they might have been just wise old women, and most of them were totally innocent. Once the mob got the idea into their heads that so-and-so was a witch, that was probably the end."

Then I remembered something.

"The marks on the gate?"

"We don't know," said Alison. "One of the villagers. Some of them know, or suspect anyway."

"And the thorns?"

"Same kind of thing. If you put thorns in a witch's footprint then she has to return to pull them out. It's a way of slowing her down."

"Oh," I said, "I see. But you don't really believe all that kind of thing, do you?"

"Of course not," said Jane, quickly, "but there's a lot of old superstitions around here that have never really died out."

"Yes," I said, "I see."

I didn't like to think, let alone, say what was in my mind then. About how Jane had come off the hill for no good reason.

"And the woman on the hill. It is the old woman from my dreams, isn't it?"

As I said it, I realised I shouldn't have said 'dreams' in the plural. As far as they knew I'd only had the one. But they didn't seem to notice.

"We think so. That dream. It's very old. None of us have ever had it, but there are stories about that dream, stories going back a long time. It's a local legend."

Another local legend, like those mysterious, unexplained deaths. There were a couple of things I had to tell Jane and Alison. The things I'd read in the extracts. I thought it was time to tell them, so I went to fetch the papers.

"Look," I said. "This bit, about Crownhill always being cursed by witches."

Jane read. Alison peered over her shoulder.

"a village long troubled by the curse of witchcraft."

"Doesn't say much really does it," said Alison.

"But look at this bit," I said. I dug out the other thing that had shocked me when I'd read it.

"The priest questioned the witch about these marks, accusing her of trying to awaken the old woman, but again the witch would say nothing."

There was silence for a long time.

"My God," said Jane eventually, "there it is. A mention of the old woman, over three hundred years ago."

"They don't talk about any strange deaths, though."

"Why would they? Life was harsher then, people probably dying all the time from disease. Even if they did think something odd was going on, they might not mention it."

"I suppose so," I said. I looked at the extracts yet again. I shivered.

"And just because you haven't found any reference to it doesn't mean they didn't think it was going on."

"Anyway," said Jane, "this is proof in itself. 'Awaken the old woman', I wonder what that means."

I didn't wonder at all. I knew. And it must have been written on my face, because Alison did something out of character. She held my hand.

"Jamie," she said, "You said 'dreams'. Has it happened again?"

I stared at the table, cursing myself for making that slip of the tongue.

"Yes," I said quietly. "Last night. That's why I had to find out what was going on."

"Oh, Jamie," said Alison. The tone of her voice was as if I was already dead.

"Alison, stop it," said Jane. She turned to me. "It doesn't mean anything. It's all a lot of superstition."

It didn't really sound like she believed what she was saying. It was, at the very least, a superstition that had lasted for over three hundred years. Possibly it was much older than that.

I ignored her, anyway.

"You shouldn't be doing it," I said, instead.

"Doing what?" asked Alison.

That was a good question.

"Whatever it is you're doing. You are doing something, aren't you?"

"No, Jamie," said Jane. "We're not. We're just trying to find out more about it, that's all. You've had a bad time and it's coming out in your mind. Asleep in the dream, then awake, like when you imagined that fire."

"I didn't imagine it," I said angrily. "It really happened!"

I didn't know what I meant by that. And I didn't know what I meant when I said, "You ought to leave it alone. Alone!"

I left the room. I knew I was acting crazily, but I couldn't

106

help it. I felt so powerless. There was not one thing I could do to stop things happening. Everything was in motion now, whether I liked it or not.

I spent some time curled up on my bed. After a while, though, I felt uncomfortable on the bed. Uneasy. I moved the papers onto the floor and the small table, and felt a little better.

Thoughts of fire kept on coming into my head. Of the fire, and Kizzie. I pushed them away and tried to concentrate on the stuff in front of me.

Piles of photocopies. Copies of old papers about Crownhill. I was trying to sort them out, putting bits about the same stuff together. It was difficult, because they were so hard to read. The writing was all squiggly and cramped, and there was a lot on every page I couldn't read. It was like reading a foreign language. I thought I'd have been doing better if it *was* in French.

Every now and again, I found another piece about the trial of the young girl. I put all these pages on my right hand side, in a pile, but it was still a very small pile compared to the mountains of paper I had around me. There were still lots of sheets I hadn't looked at even once yet. I couldn't believe that so much had been written about one tiny village. But then everywhere has its history. It was just that this place had more history than most.

When Clare arrived later on, I had a lot of questions to ask her. It was getting late. It would soon be night-time. Time to go to sleep. I felt uneasy.

107

I brought the papers down from my room and put them on the kitchen table. I showed Clare how I'd sorted them out.

"That's really good, Jamie," she said. She looked surprised.

Alison and Jane came and sat down too.

"There's all this lot here. I haven't looked at them yet. Then there's this lot; that's stuff I've looked at, but can't make head or tail of. Then this lot is boring stuff, well, boring to me anyway."

"And this?" asked Alison. She could see I was building up to it.

"That's stuff that mentions the trial of the girl. At least I think it's all the same girl. I still don't know what her name was, but it all seems to be talking about the same witch-craft trial."

"I'm really impressed," said Clare. "You don't want to come and work for me, do you?"

"Yes, that's good," said Jane. She started flicking through the pile on the trial of the girl.

"It's really hard to understand what happened," I said.

"It's always like that when you look at these things," said Clare.

"Because you're so far away in time?" asked Alison.

"Yes, but also because you don't know what you're reading is true. Take these extracts from this record. I already said that we think they were written at least ten years after the events they describe, and possibly more. So the man who wrote them may not have really known what happened anyway. He probably put these bits together from hearsay and gossip, years later. And even if he did know what was going on, it's pretty clear from some of these bits that he was convinced the girl was a witch. And if he was that biased, it makes it very hard to know what really went on."

I think I'd worked that out already, but it made sense to hear Clare say it too.

"I doubt very much that she was a witch," she added.

I wasn't so sure.

"Look at this bit," I said. "She curses the whole court."

I showed Clare the passage.

"Maybe, but you have to remember, she'd been locked up for a few days by then, hadn't she? They stopped her from sleeping for a long time. She was probably nearly out of her mind. Very often totally innocent people would crack up and start believing what they were being accused of. There's just no way of telling at this distance in time."

"Do you think she had anything to do with this boy?" I asked. "Richard Sedley. With him dying?"

"Well," said Clare, "she can't have bewitched him, because there's no such thing as witchcraft, is there?"

None of us said anything to this. Clare went on.

"But I suppose she might have poisoned him. There are these references to herbal remedies. Perhaps she *was* guilty of murder. But by poisoning, not by witchcraft."

"Do you think she did?" asked Alison.

"Again, it's impossible to tell."

"Anyway," Jane said, "even if she was a witch, they shouldn't have hanged her."

"We don't know that they did," said Clare, glancing at one of the extracts.

"But you said they didn't burn witches in this country," I said.

"No, what I mean is, we don't know that they executed her at all. We haven't found anything to say they did."

"But you said that once they started to accuse someone of being a witch, that was the end for them."

"Generally yes, but sometimes they might get let off with a series of turns in the stocks and a prison sentence. And this is a very young girl we're talking about. Sixteen, didn't you say? Well, perhaps they took pity on her. Let's hope so."

The thought that maybe she hadn't been killed cheered me up a bit. It was too awful to think that she had been, just because she was supposed to have been a witch. She was supposed to have killed this boy, Richard Sedley, with witchcraft. They'd had a quarrel, and he'd called her a witch. I wondered what they'd argued about.

I looked across the table at Alison. She'd been quiet for a while. I knew she was mooning about her friends, about how they wouldn't get her sorted out with this boy.

What else do sixteen-year old girls get upset about? Surely people have changed in three hundred years? But no. I looked at Alison and realised that people haven't changed at all. It was something like this that had happened with Richard Sedley and this witch . . . this girl; I could see it.

"Look," said Clare, "here's something about the crown."

She read.

"This year was the figure of chalk of Cronhill cleaned and repaired. For this the sum of 12d was paid to the work party."

"'12d'?" Alison asked.

"Twelve pennies," said Clare, "quite a lot of money. It must have been a big job."

"When's that from?" I asked.

"We don't know about that one, I'm afraid. Fifteen-something if the spelling's anything to go by."

"But look at the name of the village. It's Cronhill there, isn't it?"

"Yes, and the only reliable reference we have to it being called that is from 1583."

"Why do names change?"

"Who knows? Sometimes it's just a natural progression, as English itself changes. It's very rare that the name of a place is changed on purpose."

"How can things change naturally though?" I asked.

"Well, things get shortened, for a start. A really long name might get squashed up, just like we say 'thanks' or even just 'ta' for thank you. Call it sloppiness, but it's easier and quicker. Or it might be the same, but spelled differently, until people forget what it was originally called, and think it means something else."

"What sort of things?" I asked.

"Jamie, don't pester," said Jane.

111

"No, it's fine. It's good to have someone so keen," said Clare. "I don't know really, but you might just leave some letters out of a word, for example."

"Oh," I said.

I knew something. Something that had been nibbling away at the back of my mind all day. I didn't want to go to sleep. Ever again. Bad things happened to me when I was asleep.

I messed around, finding excuse after excuse to stay up a bit longer.

Finally Jane said I should go to bed.

I said I thought I ought to have a bath to relax first, so that I might sleep a bit better. I had no intention of going to bed at all, but at least this would buy me a little more time, before she started asking questions.

I ran the bath in the small bathroom that was stuck onto the back of the house, next to the kitchen. I got undressed slowly, thinking about the carving, and about the dream of the old woman. A dream that was waiting for me on the other side of sleep.

Then I realised the bathroom curtain was open, and pulled it shut against the night. It was getting quite windy outside, the weather forecast had promised storms for the next few days. It sounded as if one was brewing already. The hot water spluttered noisily into the tub, and when I thought there was enough to risk putting some cold in, I ran a little, mixing it with my hand. I turned the taps off, and got in. I sat, half listening to the wind blowing up outside and half thinking about . . . what? Just then, the

112

wind really slammed against the house for the first time. The light in the bathroom went out.

A second after it went dark, I felt a cold, wet fingernail slide down my spine. I leapt out of the bath, yelling.

I could hear Jane and Alison making noises about getting the lights back on, as I spluttered into the kitchen.

"There's . . . someone . . . something . . ." was all I got out.

"The big red switch . . . yes?" Jane was saying.

The lights went on.

"There, just the fuse again. Old house. Happens all the time."

"There's . . . someone scratched my back . . . in the bath."

I looked at Jane in terror.

"Oh yes! Happens sometimes." She smiled. "Sorry, I should have told you. It's drops of water from the beam above the bath. The steam condenses and then . . . splat! Scared the hell out of me too when we first moved here!"

Alison came in.

"There. We'll have to fix the fuse tomorrow."

She stopped when she saw me.

"You might like to get back in the bath," she said, grinning.

I did, burning with embarrassment, and not just because I'd been standing in the kitchen dripping wet with no clothes on. I sat in the bath again, and watched the drops of water form on a nail on the beam above the bath. After a couple of minutes, the drop would splash heavily into the bath.

113

I sat forward as I had been before, and waited for the next one. It hit my back. It felt just like someone scratching my spine with a wet finger. Jane was right.

I lay back in the bath, convinced I was losing it.

I began to calm down a little after a while. I chuckled to myself, thinking what an idiot I'd been to get scared like that. I decided I was being silly about the whole thing, about not wanting to go to sleep, and I felt really tired by now. I got out of the bath, and went upstairs to my room, ready to sleep.

But as soon as I closed the door behind me, the fears of the nightmare were back again, rising in my throat. Maybe it was being back in the room, in the room where I had the dreams, that did it, but I knew there was no way I was going to let myself go to sleep that night.

I went downstairs and made myself a cup of coffee, which I hate, and took it back up to my room.

I put the radio on, quietly, so Jane wouldn't hear, and sat at the small table, determined to see the night out. I sipped the coffee slowly, hoping it would start working quickly.

It didn't. I started to doze, so I found a book and tried to read for a while. But it was no good. The book was boring and was sending me to sleep even faster. I tried something else to read – the witch papers.

I found another piece about the trial that I hadn't seen before – it was horrible, how they'd made that poor girl suffer.

But even this was not enough to keep me awake. Sleep was pulling me in, and though I tried to fight it I caught myself falling asleep at the table. I jumped awake with a jolt. I got up and walked around the room, and waited for the coffee to work. Eventually it did, and a sort of half-waking buzz kept me going for a couple of hours. I read the witch trial papers, but I don't think much of it was going in.

The night moved on into the small dark hours of early morning, and I could feel myself flagging, but still the fear was too great – I couldn't let myself sleep – one glimpse of the fear of those dreams was enough to harden my resolve to stay awake. To stay away from sleep. But I was growing tired and confused. Bizarre thoughts drifted through my head.

Bad things happened to me at night, when I was asleep.

Fire.

Fire burning.

Fire burning witches.

Burning witches.

Witches.

But of course, in the end, I slept. And woke, curled up on the floor beside my bed and nothing had happened. I felt like I'd been licking a carpet for a week, and my head rang with a dull pain, but I was safe.

The witch was brought before the judge for the last time. Still she refused to answer all questions, despite the court's insistence that she in so doing was only confirming her guilt.

Then did John Sedley burst in from the back of the room, saying to the witch that he had killed her familiar with a spade and wanted to see if she was dead along with it.

At this, the witch screamed all the evil curses she could manage at John Sedley, naming him and many others as recipients of her evil magic.

Then the judge and jury were confirmed in their wise opinion of the witch's evil, and pronounced that she would be executed the day following.

10

Guilt

No dream. That was something, but I felt like death anyway that morning. It was late when I picked myself off the bedroom floor and got dressed. From downstairs came the sound of someone banging around in the kitchen.

I went down to see what was happening.

The noise was Eric, a friend of Jane's. I'd met him briefly at the Scouring. He had come to sort out the blown fuse from the night before.

There was something tickling the back of my brain as I got up and dressed. I knew I'd been thinking about something just before I'd woken up properly. I think I'd worked it, *something*, out. You know how you forget things when you actually wake up? You know it was important, but the harder you try and remember the more difficult it is. I think it was reading those papers about the trial, about the village, as I'd been trying to stay awake. I couldn't actually remember anything I'd read, perhaps I was even half-asleep as I'd read them, but something had worked itself out as I slept. The only trouble was that now I couldn't remember what it was.

Eric nodded at me as I came into the kitchen, and Jane started getting breakfast for me.

"I can do that," I protested, but she wanted to mother me so much, I gave up. Besides, I felt absolutely exhausted. I vaguely wondered if I could try and stay awake again that night. I didn't feel I had much chance of staying awake for the rest of the day.

Alison came in with some shopping.

"You don't want to know what they're saying about us in the village," she said.

"I can guess," said Jane.

"Can you?"

"The usual nasty rumours. Village gossip. That sort of thing."

"Yes. But they're also saying you gave half the village food poisoning."

"What?"

"I bumped into Susan coming back from the shop. She says people are blaming you. They say everyone who had those egg sandwiches at the Scouring is ill in bed."

"That's ridiculous!"

Alison shrugged.

"I told you not to use eggs from Fiddler's Farm, you never know how long they've been sitting around."

"But I didn't," said Jane.

Alison looked doubtful.

"Really?"

"Yes. Really. I threw them all out."

She banged a saucepan into the sink.

"So how come everyone's ill then?"

Jane shrugged. Eric banged some pipes a bit louder. I didn't see what pipes had to do with wiring.

"Just some bug or other," Jane said. She sounded tense. "Nothing to do with us."

"Susan's absolutely flat out," Alison went on. "Already been to five houses this morning. All got the same thing."

Jane ignored her and did some furious washing up.

Eric stopped what he was doing.

"So you're the Crownhill killer, then?" he smirked.

"Don't be stupid," said Jane crossly, "those deaths have happened for hundreds of years."

Eric looked shocked. I shivered.

"Just joking, Janey. Steady on, eh?"

"No, Eric, it's not a joke," said Jane. She seemed really worked up, not like her at all. "The people who have died were poor, weak, people. People under stress, people without anyone to look after them, unloved people, unwanted people. It has nothing to do with my cooking! My cooking is perfectly safe!"

There was an uneasy silence. Eric stared at Jane, more surprised I think, than hurt. I stared at the floor, in that embarrassed way you do when someone loses their temper. But also I was wondering if Jane really knew all that about the peculiar deaths, or if it was just guesswork.

Then Alison started laughing. Jane turned.

"What's so funny?" she said.

"Well," said Alison, still giggling, "there was that time you set light to the bin bag with burning toast."

There was another uneasy pause, and then Jane started laughing too. Eric dared a smile, and so did I.

"That's not possible, is it?" Eric asked, chuckling.

Alison just pointed at her mum, and shrugged her shoulders.

We laughed.

Eric went back to what he was doing. I knew he had been joking, but I didn't like to think about what might be the actual cause of all those strange deaths that had happened over the years in Crownhill.

Jane and Alison were still talking about the village rumours, but in a more friendly way now.

"Mum, calm down. It's just gossip. Anyway, it's not everyone. Susan said it was mostly Mrs Vickers at the Post Office."

"Mrs Vickers?" asked Eric. "The old crone."

I dropped my spoon. My hands were shaking that badly. I guess it was because I was so exhausted.

Everyone looked at me.

"Where's Clare?" I asked Jane nervously. I felt so tired, but a lurking fear was growing in my insides, and began to shake the sleep from me.

"Why?"

"I need to ask her something."

It was what Eric had said . . . I needed to ask Clare something.

"But she's gone."

"Gone? She can't have gone. Not now."

"Back to London. She might come back in a week or two."

"Why, Jamie?" asked Alison.

I stopped. I stared at Alison.

"That word."

"Which word?" she asked impatiently.

"Crone. What does it mean? Exactly."

"Well, its just what you call a nasty woman, isn't it?"

"What sort of woman?"

"Well . . . an old one, a nasty old woman."

"Eric wandered over.

"A bit of a witch. That's what it means."

"Don't you see?" I said. It was so obvious, I couldn't believe no one had seen it before.

"Crownhill. It never used to be called that. And that was never a crown on the hill, was it? The village used to be called Cronhill, and the thing on the hill used to be an old woman."

"So?"

"So remember how Clare said you might lose a letter from a name? How the spelling could change? Crownhill used to be called Cronhill, and before that it used to be . . ." I didn't want to say it myself, out loud.

"Just add an 'e'," I said.

Alison looked at Jane.

"Cronehill," said Jane quietly. "Crone hill. The Witch Hill."

"Bloody hell," said Eric. "Make us some coffee, Janey, will you?"

Eric drank his coffee quickly, then said he'd need to come back later; he'd forgotten something. Jane showed him out.

I so wanted to tell Clare, to see if she thought I was right. Somehow from the look on Jane's face, I knew I was. It made absolute sense. It fitted. But then why had the village got a new name? Did the villagers change the name of their village, and the carving on the hill at the same time? If they had, why would they do that? I suppose it's not very nice living somewhere called after a witch, but why had they changed the name? And why then?

But perhaps it had just happened, was *still* happening naturally, like Clare said, over time.

"There's something else," I said, over a cup of coffee. I thought I might have to get used to drinking the foul stuff.

"What's that?" asked Alison. She came round to look at the paper I was holding. It was the undated piece about the Crown being cleaned.

"This year was the figure of chalk of Cronhill cleaned and repaired. For this the sum of 12d was paid to the work party."

"What about it?"

"This is from somewhere in the fifteen hundreds. Maybe a hundred years before the Civil War, and the trial of the girl, and possibly the name changing. Notice it doesn't call the crown a crown. It says a 'figure of chalk'. That doesn't sound like a crown to me. It sounds like a person."

"Maybe," said Jane, "but with this old way of speaking it's hard to tell."

Alison looked at me. I could tell she thought I was very near the truth.

"You think that up until the war, the village was called Cronehill, or Cronhill, and it was changed to 'crown' at some point after that, and the carving with it."

"That *could* make sense," said Jane. "If the king was back. After the Restoration, I mean, when the monarchy was restored to power. And they wanted to show their loyalty to the king. Then they could forget about the witch."

"Or try to forget, anyway," I said.

"And they re-carved the old witch on the hill to try and make her look like a crown?"

"Maybe they didn't have to. Perhaps it already looked such a mess by then that all they needed to do was add a few lines and *call* it a crown. Perhaps they even believed it themselves."

Alison looked at the copy of the old document again.

"You said it was undated, Jamie," she said.

"It is," I said.

"Well, there's no year, but there *is* a date. Look here."

She pointed to a particularly crabby, cramped bit of writing.

"Can you read that?"

"I think it says 'May eve'," I said.

"That's precisely what it says."

Jane drew breath.

"What?" I said.

"May eve. Walpurgisnacht," Alison said, almost laughing. She was delighted with this for some reason. "The eve

125

of Beltane. The number one time in the year for witchy activity!"

"Alison," said Jane. There was a warning tone in her voice.

"What?" I said, again.

"Well, that's quite a coincidence," Alison said, ignoring her mother. "If you believe in coincidences, that is."

"Why?"

"Because May eve is today. The thirtieth of April."

It was much later that day. Alison sat across the table from me. I was barely managing to keep awake by this point. Last night had caught up with me. A thought kept nagging at my mind. I kept trying to push it away but I couldn't completely. A thought about the night that was coming. The eve of May Day.

"I'm going to ring Rebecca," Alison said. From the way she said it, I knew this was crunch time. After a moment or two, I heard her voice from the hall, where the phone was. She didn't sound happy, but there were more serious things worrying me.

I wondered how far back in time those inexplicable deaths in the village went. Everyone said they were real; that they had really happened. They also said that they had been happening down the centuries. As long ago as the time of the young girl tried for witchcraft and Richard Sedley?

But perhaps it was just a load of nonsense. Old wives' tales.

Jane came back in.

"Doesn't sound good, does it," I said.

"What?"

"Alison."

"Oh. Oh dear," she said, pulling a face, "doesn't it?"

The sound of Alison running upstairs to her bedroom confirmed it.

"There's so little I can do for her, now. She's nearly grown-up, and we're stuck out here when she wants to be in town with her friends. They're all getting boyfriends now. I'm glad you two are getting on. She needs friends." Are we getting on? I thought. I felt a bit awkward; I said nothing and let her go on.

"Do you think I make things worse, James?"

"Of course not," I said.

How would I know? I thought.

"With all this business about the hill. She loves helping me, but I think it puts her apart from her friends even more."

"No," I said, simply. I couldn't think of anything cleverer to say, but Jane looked grateful nonetheless.

"Anyway," I went on, "it's too important. It's something she really believes in, isn't it?"

"Yes. You're right. For a while I just thought she was doing it to support me. Since her father left we've stuck by each other; done everything together. Now I know she's really into it, for herself. But sometimes you have to let things go a bit, make allowances for other people. Especially if they don't understand what you're doing. I don't think Alison's very good at that."

127

"You mean, if you want to keep your friends?"

"Yes," Jane said. "People can find something they don't understand frightening. They can end up hating it, for that alone."

Suddenly I realised that what Jane was saying could apply equally well to another sixteen-year-old girl I knew. Or knew of, anyway.

"Do you think her friends will end up hating her?" I asked.

"I don't think it will come to that. A few tears, on both sides, and she and Rebecca will be fine again."

But what if Alison was a sixteen-year-old during the witch-craze?

I was suddenly filled with a horrible pain. The pain of despair. A huge loneliness swept into me, a feeling of being absolutely isolated. As isolated as I'd been that night when the fire swept through my home, but this was even worse, if possible, because it was a feeling of being alone against a world that *hated* you, that didn't understand you. That was coming to get you.

And the pain was coming from right where I was. An old lingering hurt that had festered for hundreds of years. It was coming from within the house itself.

There was a knock at the back door.

It was Eric.

"You ought to pay someone who knows what they're doing," he said.

Jane smiled, and let him back into the kitchen.

"I just thought you might be able to stop it happening. It quite scared poor Jamie here, last night."

Eric paused for a second to look at me. He didn't say anything, and then he went on with his work.

"I'm not an electrician, and the wiring in this place is a joke. It must be ancient."

"Don't be silly. It might be old, but it's not ancient."

"I'm not being silly. It could be dangerous. I'm going to have to have this whole unit off the wall, to check the wiring. It looks very dodgy where it goes through the panelling."

And so they went on. Eric got a big hammer out and started to lever bits of the fuse cupboard off.

"Hey, do you have to do that?" Jane protested.

"Yes, I do," said Eric, testily.

I stopped listening.

The telephone rang, a short, brash, modern sound that got my attention.

"Yes? Oh hello," said Jane into the phone, but again I wasn't really listening. I was thinking about a girl. Not much older than Alison, she had been tried for being a witch.

"Jamie?" said. "Your mum's on the phone."

"Oh," I said. I suddenly felt very tired again.

"Speak to her, Jamie," she said. "Just to stop her worrying."

I hesitated. Jane waited patiently, but even so I felt I was being put under pressure. Still Jane didn't say anything. She just looked at me steadily and then smiled.

"Okay," I said quietly.

I spoke to Mum for a while.

"How are you?" she said. I could tell she was trying not to fuss, but failing.

"I'm fine," I said. I felt . . . flat.

"Dad says hello. He says it won't be long before you can come back up. Everything's getting sorted out much quicker than we hoped."

"Oh," I said, "everything's all right then, is it?"

I meant to sound sarcastic. I couldn't help it.

"You know I don't mean that. Kizzie . . ."

"Don't talk to me about Kiz," I shouted, "You don't understand!"

"Kizzie . . ."

"I said stop it!"

I really yelled. Mum was quiet. Jane came rushing in, and Eric, startled by the uproar, turned on his stepladder and fell against one of the kitchen walls. He was holding the large hammer, and it flailed across the wall as he fell. Jane and I watched as he went down.

"Are you all right?" said Jane, running across to him.

"Yes," he mumbled, "But you'd better get someone else in."

"Are you all right?" Mum asked me down the phone.

"Yes," I said, "but I'm going now."

"Why? Are you hurt? What was that noise?"

"That was a man falling off a ladder. I'm fine."

I hung up.

I was staring at the mess. Not the mess of Eric on the floor, but something else.

"I think you're going to need a plasterer, too. Sorry Jane," said Eric.

He was right. A huge section of old plaster had just dropped off the kitchen wall.

"As long as you're all right."

"Just look at that though."

"No," I said, "Just look at *that*."

I pointed, and Jane and Eric followed my gaze to the bare old wall, the wall that had been hidden behind the old plaster.

The lower half was covered in drawings. Faint, dull red drawings. Not really drawings, but symbols and letters. Even what looked like an odd word in strange lettering. They looked very old.

Somehow I was not surprised to see them there. It made sense. What did surprise me was the series of other marks on the wall. They started at waist height and disappeared out of sight where the kitchen ceiling began. They were the unmistakable scorch marks of fire. Thick dirty sooty black marks.

"There was never a fireplace there, was there?" Eric asked.

Jane shook her head.

"Not that I know of."

"Weird," said Eric. "And as for that little lot."

He nodded at the drawings, as if he was afraid to even move his hand out towards them. We all knew what sort of thing they were, even if we didn't know exactly what they meant.

"Give me that, will you?"

Jane took the hammer from Eric. I thought she was going to take more of the plaster off in the kitchen, but she went upstairs to the spare room; my room, which was the one directly above the kitchen.

Eric and I followed her.

She swung the hammer gently against the plaster. It was very old and dry and fell off easily.

Alison came in from her room then. She looked as if she'd been crying.

"What on earth are you doing, Mum?" she asked.

Everyone ignored her.

Jane kept swinging the hammer against the wall until there was a three-foot square hole.

"No more, then?" asked Eric. He seemed anxious.

"No," said Jane, "Just more of that."

She waved her hand. Every inch of brick that she'd exposed was charred.

"Must have been some fire," said Eric.

"Yes," said Jane. "Real heat to scorch brick like this."

I went cold.

This was something I knew about.

I knew what it was like to see your house go up in smoke. From the inside. I wondered if anyone had died in this fire. I wondered if anyone had been stuck, trapped by the fire at the top of the stairs. Someone like my little sister. Like Kizzie.

"Kizzie," I said quietly, tears starting to burn my eyes.

Jane saw me and looked at Eric.

"Come and sit down, Jamie," she said. "Alison, can you show Eric out?"

Eric went downstairs without a word, with Alison following, but I wasn't watching them. I stared at the blackened old wall in the bedroom.

"Kizzie," I said again. Louder.

Jane took my arm, but I shrugged her off.

"Jamie, come on."

"No!" I yelled. "I'm fed up with being told I'm all right!"

"Jamie!"

"I'm not! I'm not all right! I didn't save her!" I screamed, and fell sobbing to the floor.

Jane held me while I cried. She waited a long time. She told me to breathe, slowly and deeply, but she didn't tell me it would be all right, and I was grateful to her for that. At last, the tears stopped, and I sat up. Jane took me and sat me on my bed. She held my face in her hands.

"No, Jamie," she said. She spoke calmly but firmly. "No, *you* didn't save her."

I started to shake my head.

"But I should have. I was there, at the end of the hall, with her. I thought she was with Mum and Dad."

"I know, but it was dark and noisy and confusing, how were you to know that Kizzie had chosen that night to be the first night she didn't join your parents in bed? You didn't, you couldn't have known she was still at your end of the house."

She waited for me to answer. I didn't.

"Just leave me alone," I said, after a while. "Please?"

She went. I heard her talking to Alison downstairs. Alison was crying again. I could even make out some of what they were saying. Her friend *had* asked that boy out, but not for Alison. She had asked him for herself. Now Alison had lost a friend, too. She sounded so miserable; the sound of her sobbing filled my room as if she was there. It

133

filled the whole house. And with it, that feeling of aching loneliness returned. A feeling of complete emptiness. The complete absence of comfort or kindness. It began to eat into me, to destroy me. I could feel myself weakening beneath it. The weight of this pain was just too much for me, for anyone to bear. I thought about Kizzie again. Again and again and again.

I would never forgive myself.

Yes.

No.

Jane was right.

I hadn't saved her. *I* hadn't.

But someone else had.

That was all. My little sister was still alive; she was with Mum and Dad. But no thanks to me. Right now, probably, they'd be putting her to bed. She'd just have had a bath, and maybe a bedtime story, and they'd be putting her to bed in the guesthouse bedroom.

But for all I knew she could be dead. I hadn't seen her. She was too little to speak on the phone. She might as well be dead.

She could have been dead. The fact she wasn't, that she was all right; it wasn't because of me.

The fire.

I'd jumped out of the window. I thought Kizzie was with them, with Mum and Dad. But for the first time in her short little life, she hadn't wandered through from her room to join them in the middle of the night. Mum and

Dad were probably having the best night's sleep they'd had since *I* was little. They didn't know she wasn't there.

It was so dark and bright and smoke was everywhere, and I couldn't breathe. There was thick, black, rolling smoke throughout the house, lit only by the evil orange light from the fire itself. I was scared and I just wanted to get out.

I smashed a window.

The other landing window burst inwards. A fireman shoved his head through.

"Don't jump kid! Wait for me!" he said.

Or something like that.

I ignored him. I was too scared, and I could see the ground outside. I knew I would be all right, and I jumped.

The ground hit me hard. I felt my leg go, but I was safe.

Mum and Dad ran up from the front of the house.

"Where's Kizzie?" shouted Dad.

Mum screamed. A sound like I'd never heard anyone make. Let alone my mum. It was a sound from the bottom of her being, from the pit, a sound born out of total horror.

"KIZZIE!"

And yes, the fireman got her, just in time. Her room was furthest from where the fire had started and she was sleeping happily, unaware of anything.

But I had left her. She might have died.

The pain was too much; thinking about Kizzie, and Alison, and the pain welling up from this ancient cottage was just too much to bear.

And now, perversely, I longed for sleep.

Even if it might mean the worst.

Because it might mean the worst.

I longed for sleep to come and take the pain away. To grow numb, to forget, and maybe never to wake again.

I lay on my bed, and then it all began. For real.

Then did the witch exercise some more of her foul magic arts. She summoned friends, and demons from the other world, which opened the door of her prison cell, having first removed the guards placed there by the righteous villagers.

The witch fled to her mother's cottage, and there she was seen to pause at the gate, where she spied the dead cat, her familiar, Chub. She then took the animal into the house, without doubt to practise more of her magic work over the body of her dead familiar, uttering unknown words of incantations and spells.

Now a crowd had gathered on the hill, but hearing that the witch was retreated to her house, they began to grow angry. They came off the hill, to pursue this wicked young witch. But she had locked the door to her cottage with magic, and so one of the villagers did call to her, saying that they had the rope ready for her neck and that she should come out to greet it.

But she did not come out.

11

The Dream

Such beauty. I have never seen anything like it before. After all those wicked black nights, now there floats before me the face of such a beautiful girl. A woman. Long, dark, nearly black hair that reaches to beyond her shoulders. Dark, chocolate brown eyes. Red, red lips. Lips that are smiling at me. Who is this woman? I don't care. After all the horror, the pain, the anger, this is a happy thing. Such a beautiful moment, a moment that will see me through all that is to come.

I wished for numbness and I wished to forget, but this is so much better. It reminds me that I want to be alive, that things will be all right again. Some day.

The woman takes a step towards me. She is wearing a gown of rich dark blue silk. Dark blue like the night sky. Sewn into it are gold threads. The gold embroidery forms some sort of strange pattern, but I cannot see what. It does not matter. A huge wave of beautiful calm sweeps into me as I look at her. The calmness grows and grows and begins to transform itself into happiness. I am so happy that I cannot help smiling. It feels like the first time I have ever smiled. It feels wonderful. The happiness grows.

The woman smiles at me, and my smile becomes a laugh. I am laughing from relief, from joy, from wonder.

"Who are you?" I ask, but she shakes her head.

It does not matter. That's what she means. She is right; it does not matter, and I do not care.

She takes another step towards me. Her eyes are telling me things. That I am going to be all right, that I am good, that the pain will go. I let her tell me this and let myself relax. I let myself be happy.

It feels so wonderfully good.

She takes a third step towards me.

She holds out her hand towards me, and I touch her. I look at her hand in mine.

And her hand is old, and shrunken.

I look up and I am looking into the face of the witch.

She opens her toothless mouth. I know she is thinking of the worst thing she can say. The thing that will scare me the most.

I cannot tell you what she says.

The words gurgle from her foul throat, and slip out between her withered lips.

I feel my guts turn over.

I am trapped. With her, in her foul dark hole inside the hill.

But I run!

Though the underground tunnels of her lair, I run

142

madly. I know she is behind me. I can hear her scrabbling after me. It sounds pathetic, but I also know how disgustingly fast she can move.

I get to the ladder that leads up the shaft out of her smelly pit. As I put my first foot onto it, I realise that it is made from the rib bones and leg bones of a hundred men. Some of the bones are not that old. I know this because there is still flesh dropping off them.

I grab the first bone in my hands and start to climb. Before I am even halfway up, she is at the bottom, scuttling after me.

For every one of the bone steps I take, she somehow takes three. The light, the tiny dim circle of light at the top of the shaft seems no more than the size of a coin. I keep climbing, but the bone stairway starts to give way. Every rung I put my feet on drops away from me. Then suddenly I am grasping for clumps of grass at the top of the shaft. Lumps of chalk and soil come away in my hand, but I haul myself half out of the hole. I realise that if the ladder of bones has given way, then maybe she will not be able to follow me.

I feel a bony claw-hand grab my ankle.

I kick back, desperately, and get myself a little further out of the hole, praying that this nightmare will stop.

All I can think of is the safety of my room. My room in the cottage. The thought of it gives me enough extra strength to pull myself free of the hole. I feel the witch's fingernails scratch my ankle as I pull free.

I am on the hill.

I know it is midnight. The sky is the deepest black curtain of night, and yet glows an eerie pallid blue colour too. The trees glow a lurid green. There is not a breath of wind. There is not a sound, until I hear a croak from the hole, and remember the witch. I flee down the hill, towards the cottage.

As I run I vaguely realise I am running over the carving of the witch. I realise for the first time that I have bare feet, and I realise that this is how the chalk got on my feet. I have *always* known it, but it is happening now.

The hill drops away from me, and as I run the ground thuds into my feet. My bad leg starts to ache again, and my knees are burning with a pain from each blow into the ground.

The slope drops away sharper, and I lose my footing. I half-fall, half-roll a long way down the hill. At last I hit something, and stop. For a moment, I black out. When I come round, I am in bed. My bed, in the cottage.

Safe. I am where I wanted to be. But then I feel something is with me.

I know that I am not safe. Quite the reverse. This is just where *she* wanted me to be. *In this room.* She wanted me to come back here.

It is dark, but there is just enough light from the moon to see the witch.

She is sitting on my chest. She has got me at last, and though it took three dreams to get me, and though I wriggle like a hooked fish, she *has* got me. She sits on my chest and though she is as light as a feather, I feel her start to get heavier.

144

I cannot move. I cannot breathe.

I know now that she will kill me. And I know how she will kill me.

Just like Richard Sedley had met *his* strange death.

She will stop me breathing, just like that thick black smoke that tried to stop me before.

She opens her foul mouth. She is laughing again.

"You didn't save her," she gurgles, grinning. "You didn't save her."

Vaguely, I wonder what it was she tormented Richard Sedley with as she killed him. But then the witch laughs and as she does so she gets heavier and heavier. And I want to scream, but I cannot, and I want to shout at her but I cannot. All I can do is suffocate, while floods of tears pour down my face, as she laughs at me.

By this hour had darkness fallen on the village, but a crowd remained outside the witch's cottage, now with lanterns and torches so they might see that the witch did not escape.

They began to grow righteously angry, and a great disturbance and tumult arose among the people. A shout went up for the witch to come out of her lair, but she did not do so.

Then a young man stepped forward saying that the witch had to be punished. He did take a torch from his neighbour, and put it to the thatch on the cottage. Then he threw the torch in at the window.

It was thus that the place was set afire.

12

. . . *Something Wicked This Way Comes*

Time closes in.

As my death nears, as *my* time runs out, *all of time* is squashed into this tiny moment. The moment when the witch kills me. Each breath I squeeze in now is perhaps my very last, and each one takes forever.

The witch sits on my chest. She has been silent for what seems like a long time now, but is probably only a few seconds. A strange calm has settled on us, while she waits for me to stop breathing altogether.

I try to puke, but the weight of her on me is so great that I cannot even do that.

Silent tears burn down my cheeks as I gasp another breath into me.

How many more now? How few?

The witch gets bored again with just waiting for me to suffocate, and decides to try and scare me to death as well. She turns her white skin purple. I mean shocking, deep, strong purple. Her whole face is as bright as a berry. Then

149

she turns her skin black; blacker than coal. Just her sickly eyes peep through the night-slit of her face. Then she decides to make herself green. Not the healthy green of spring grass, but sludge, scum, green decay. Then she gets bored with these tricks, and makes herself white again. That sick, translucent, death whiteness.

I let out another silent, breathless scream.

Time closes in. And I think about something else again. Someone else, again. Poor girl, I think. She has no friends. Her friends have left her. Maybe they hate her. They don't understand her, because she messes around with herbs and potions and other strange things.

I gasp another pathetic amount of air into me. Time folds in on itself some more.

Poor girl. Alone in this room, while outside the villagers are gathering, angry. It is nothing that she has done, that they are angry. They are just angry and want to take it out on someone. A scapegoat. Anyone will do. A woman. A girl. A boy. Someone to blame for their own unhappi-nesses.

The real evil goes unnoticed, of course. The real evil is sitting on me, taking my air away from me, taking my life away from me. I try another little gasp; I manage a bit, but I don't think there will be many more. Not now.

Poor boy. Alone in this room. To be here in this tiny space, just underneath the thatch. Hunted, hated. While the real evil sits in her hole in the hill, laughing at it all. Someone innocent will die, again.

The real cause will escape, again.

Time has collapsed completely, now.

There is no difference between then and now. It is all one.

There is a crowd outside the cottage. There are lots of voices. A big crowd, then. The voices sound angry. The sound grows louder; more people are coming to see what is going on.

What are they doing here? Fire. It is all to do with fire. I see that now, from where I lie gasping under the witch. Not hanging. Fire.

A shout comes from outside. The voices sound angry, and even a little afraid, too. They do not know what to do, but things are out of control now.

Then there comes a smell that I would recognise, if I were able to draw any breath into me.

The smell of burning fills the bedroom. Just a little at first, but getting stronger and stronger. Now I do recognise the smell. It is unmistakable. I have smelled it before, though it was slightly different last time. This is the smell of straw and wood burning, not plastic and vinyl.

I know what is coming, but the girl does not. She runs to the door, still clutching the body of her dead cat in her arms. The tears have not yet dried on her face. I try to tell her not to open the door, but it is too late. She lifts the heavy wooden catch on the door, and the flames leap in at her before it is even halfway open.

She screams.

Don't! I think. You need the air for breathing, not screaming.

I know that so clearly, with the witch stopping *me* from having any.

But the girl cannot know I am with her, and she does not stop screaming. She runs round the room madly. Smoke is funnelling in through holes in the thatch above her head.

The window! The window! I think.

She does not even seem to think about trying it. She knows what I do not, that the shutters are stuck and will not open.

The house burns? I know why the girl was *not* hanged, then.

I try in vain once more to wriggle out from under the witch, but she is as heavy as I am nearly dead. The closer to death I get, the heavier she becomes.

Am I really going to die? I think. Why?

In me, somewhere deep inside me, the anger starts. Pain, I have plenty of that. And it only takes a slight switch for pain to become anger. All the hurt and pain comes welling up out of me in a rush, as I think about Kizzie, as I watch the girl burn, and it scares me. This amount of rage should kill me, but it doesn't.

And instead, I do something with it. I summon up the strength to do one last thing. I bring time together. In the room, the girl's room, my room, there is something I am

152

more afraid of than anything. This thing scares me even more than the witch does.

But I am going to use it. It is going to help me.

Fire.

"Witch," I croak.

She stops her laughing and peers down at me. She seems surprised. That I am still alive, I suppose.

"Witch," I hiss, "Look at yourself. You're on fire. Didn't you know?"

It is true. The fire has leapt from door, to thatch, to beam, to girl, to cat's body, to her bed, to *my* bed, to me, *to the witch*.

I have done it.

The witch looks at me in horror.

Yes, she is scared. But not of me. Not of me. She is scared of the fire. And her fear gives me hope, and I begin to grow stronger again.

Her smelly rags catch in a second. Her oily hair is alight a moment later. She burns, and as she does so, she gets lighter. She starts to thrash about on top of me. I can see she still wants to kill me, but it is no use. She will have to forget about me. With every second she gets lighter and lighter. She is burning. She falls from me onto the floor. She flaps at herself, trying to put the flames out, but she is only fanning the fire. I could have told her that.

From the bed I look down at the floor. I think I can see two figures rolling in flames; old witch, young girl.

The girl is trying to take the witch with her.

For a second I cannot move. The weight on me was so

great, and I think my lungs have stopped working. I am paralysed. There is not enough air again. I must conserve air. The air is still going, even though the witch is gone too.

I sit up, then, with a shock.

Oh no, I think, not again.

The room is on fire. The cottage is on fire.

I can hear a crowd outside, voices shouting. They do not know what to do. It is out of control.

Far away I hear the wail of a fire engine. I know that sound. It is a sound of my time.

The fire is real. But this time I know what to do.

I pull my door open.

Yes. The fire is in the hallway. I knew it would be. At least the lights haven't gone yet. By some miracle, the ropy old electrics are still okay. And the stairs are clear, but there is fire between the top of the stairs and Alison's room. I have no idea where Jane is.

"Alison!" I yell. "Jane!"

I have no idea what time it is. I have no idea how long I have been asleep. I do not know where my aunt and cousin are, but then I hear shouts from one of the other bed-rooms.

I am scared, but I have lived with fire for so long now, every waking moment, and most of my sleeping ones, that I know what to do. I grab a blanket from my bed and run down the stairs to the bathroom. For some reason the fire is only upstairs.

In a few seconds I have thrown the blanket in the bath and soaked it with water. I run back upstairs.

Alison's door opens. There is the fire, waiting for me, between me and her. She screams.

"It's all right!" I yell.

I throw the soaking blanket over me like a cape, but covering my head too, and run. I run straight through the fire, and I am with Alison.

"Where's your mum?" I shout.

Alison is scared. Too scared to talk. I kick Jane's bedroom door open. It is empty; she must be downstairs somewhere.

It is time to go.

I grab Alison by the shoulders.

"Just run when I do!" I yell. "Okay?"

She nods, dimly aware of what I am saying.

"Alison! Jamie!"

It is Jane, calling from downstairs. I can tell from the sound in her voice that she is panicking badly. Her voice sounds just like Mum's did, last time. I know she doesn't know what to do. That she will do nothing. But at least she is safe, downstairs, away from the fire for the moment.

I look at Alison, trying to decide whether she knows what I want her to do. Then I throw the blanket over both of our heads, and we go. Clinging to each other, we leap through the flames pouring out of the bedroom. The blanket is too small for both of us, and I feel a lick of heat on my legs, but we are through.

We have come through the fire, unhurt.

Then, in panic, we practically fall down the stairs.

It is said that not long after this time that the name of this place was changed by agreement with all the village folk.

It is said that they had had enough of all things to do with the evil of witchcraft.

It is said that they wished to forget what they had done to the girl, Alyson Greaves, in the name of good.

Epilogue

After all that, it was all familiar ground to me. I know about what happens when your house burns down in the night. I know about the terror, and then the relief, but the guilt and the questions . . .

And I know about the crowd that's waiting outside. They've been watching and waiting, but not actually doing anything to help. And when they see you come out and they're almost disappointed and they don't look you in the eye, I know all about that too.

And I know about trips to hospital in the dark, just to see that everyone's all right from the smoke and the shock.

"Any idea what started it?"

"That old wiring."

"Mum, you can't blame Eric."

"I'm not. It was probably me. I might have damaged it with that hammer."

I knew what had started the fire.

159

I had.

I only hoped it had burned the evil out of the hill, too. For good, this time. For the moment, there was no way of knowing.

Time would tell.

My leg wasn't too bad. They kept me in overnight. I'd twisted it in the first fire, but I'd got it burnt this time. It was a small price to pay.

Jane wouldn't leave me alone. Nor Alison. They both came visiting next morning. I was out of bed, hobbling around the ward when the nurse wasn't there to tell me not to.

"Jamie, you were wonderful! Just brilliant!"

I shrugged it all off, but it sort of helped. It was nice, in fact.

"He just didn't hesitate," Jane explained to the nurse, "knew what to do straight away. I was useless. But Jamie was fantastic!"

She went on, and on. But I let her. I could have told her that things are easier when you've had practice, that I wasn't going to mess up a second chance to get things right, but I didn't.

I watched Jane and Alison, as if I wasn't there. They were laughing and joking easily with each other, and I knew something had happened for them. Things like that, like the fire, can really make you realise what matters most.

And then the doors at the end of the ward opened, and I saw Mum and Dad come through. I didn't see Kiz. She

160

wasn't tall enough for me to see her over the nurse's desk, but I heard her.

"Ja-mie?" she called, like we were playing hide and seek.

The little thing. She had no idea of what had happened to her, to me, to any of us. It was all a big game for her; another fun thing to do in life's unending stream of fun things to do.

The nurse was still checking Mum and Dad in, but Kizzie had poked her head around the desk and had seen me.

She ran over to me, all two and a half years of her, and I swept her up in my arms, crying and crying like I would never stop.

"Jamie?" she asked.

"Yes, Kiz," I said, "it's all right. It's all okay now."

I squeezed her so hard she started to giggle.

"Jamie?" she asked, again.

"What, Kizzie?" I said, smiling and crying, "what is it?"

"Jamie, shall we hop like a bunny?"

It was the longest sentence I'd ever heard her say.

"Yes, please," I said, and as Mum and Dad came over, laughing, I began to hop round the floor of the ward with my baby sister.

Also by Marcus Sedgwick

Floodland

Imagine that England is covered by water, and Norwich is an island . . .

Zoe, left behind in the confusion when her parents escaped, survives there as best she can. Alone and desperate among marauding gangs, she manages to dig a derelict boat out of the mud and gets away to Eels Island. But Eels Island, whose raggle-taggle inhabitants are dominated by the strange boy Dooby, is full of danger too.

The belief that she will one day find her parents spurs Zoe on to a dramatic escape in an exciting story set in a watery England, as it could be a few years from now.

"A compelling first novel, demanding but rewarding" *The Scotsman*

"an engrossing drama" *Books for Keeps*

"a terrifying but unforgettable story of great courage, kindness and hope" *Parents' Guide*

"Great stuff" *The Daily Telegraph*